Chioniso

and other stories

Chioniso

and other stories

by

Shimmer Chinodya

WEAVER
PRESS

Published by Weaver Press, Box A1922, Avondale, Harare. 2012
<www.weaverpresszimbabwe.com>

The following stories are reprinted here: 'Queues' (*Writing Still*, 2003) 'Tavonga' (*Writing Now*, 2005) 'Last Laugh' (*Laughing Now*, 2007). All three anthologies were published by Weaver Press.

Typeset by Weaver Press
Photograph of Shimmer Chinodya
© Weaver Press
Cover Design: Danes Design, Harare.
Printed by: Benaby Printing and Publishing (Pvt) Ltd., Harare.

ISBN: 978-1-77922-170-4

SHIMMER CHINODYA was born in Gweru, Zimbabwe, in 1957, the second child in a large, happy family. He studied English Literature and Education at the University of Zimbabwe. After a spell in teaching and in curriculum development, he proceeded to the Iowa Writers' Workshop (USA) where he earned an MA in Creative Writing.

His first novel, *Dew in the Morning* (1982) was written when he was eighteen. This was followed by *Farai's Girls* (1984), *Child of War* (under the pen name B.Chirasha, 1986), *Harvest of Thorns* (1989), *Can We Talk and other stories* (1998), *Tale of Tamari* (2004), *Chairman of Fools* (2005), *Strife* (2006), and *Tindo's Quest* (2011). His work appears in numerous anthologies, including *Soho Square* (1992), *Writer's Territory* (1999), *Tenderfoots* (2001), *Writing Still* (2004), *Writing Now* (2005) and *Laughing Now* (2007). He has also written children's books, educational texts, training manuals, radio and film scripts, including one for the award-winning feature film, *Everyone's Child*. He has won many awards, including the Commonwealth Writers Prize (Africa Region) and a NOMA Honourable mention for *Harvest of Thorns*, and subsequently the NOMA award for Strife, and a Caine Prize shortlist for 'Can we Talk'. He has won the Zimbabwe Book Publishers Association Awards on many occasions, and won the National Arts Council's NAMA award for *Strife* and *Tale of Tamari*. He has also received many fellowships abroad and from 1995 to 1997 was Distinguished DANA Professor in Creative Writing and African Literature at the University of St Lawrence in upstate New York.

His novels, *Harvest of Thorns* and *Strife* have been translated and published n Germany.

Contents

Martha's Hero

'Did anyone see you come?' he whispered.

Earnestly, she shook her head.

A bat skimmed away from the darkening trees on the ridge and over his head. Feeling the thermal, and never one to be caught off guard, he instinctively reached for the muzzle of his AK 47.

Then, he shuffled his hand inside the large plastic bag that she'd brought him containing his clothes – a pair of jeans, two T-shirts, socks, washed, freshly pressed and still reeking of village soap, matches and two twenty-packs of cigarettes.

'Did you wash and iron the clothes yourself, as I told you?'

'Yes, yes, Comrade.'

'Sure?'

'Yes, Comrade Ponda.'

He was half a head taller than her and perhaps no more than three years older. Now, as he guided her youthful face into his opened shirt with recently acquired confidence, he could feel her breath rising and her body squirming in his grip.

'Comrade, no,' she pleaded, but he ignored her, stroking her raw-avocado-pear-firm breasts and clawing hungrily at her slender thighs. His hands were hardened like wood, after seasons of hauling crates of ammo, scraping the unyielding earth to lay landmines or burying dead comrades. He raised her face to his and as he began to feed at her mouth, she detected the tang of cigarettes mixed with the sweet odour of marijuana.

She whimpered.

'How are fighters like us supposed to survive, lonely in the bush while you're all safely tucked away in schools?' he muttered angrily.

'Comrade, no!'

It was a cry not of pleasure but of fear and pain.

***

Later when he released her, a three-quarter yellow moon was struggling out of the sluggish horizon of huts in the east. He had instructed her to keep to the edge of the forest to avoid the Rhodesian forces, and the curfew, but now the dogs sensed her from the village and barked furiously. Would she be spotted and shot at? Would her sister Winnie and her daughter hear her arrive?

The pain between her legs was searing, as if she had been sliced with a new razor blade. She felt hollow, used, as if her insides would collapse. She sweated and shivered at the same time. Her dress was sticky. She feared she was leaving a thin trail, an almost invisible trickle of blood, all the way from the ridge: just like a wounded animal being stalked by a beast of prey, or perhaps some cursed unit of Rhodesian troops. She wiped the sweat from her forehead and dragged herself on. She stumbled into a thorn bush, and heard her dress rip.

What if she stepped on a snake or a booby trap nesting in the grass?

And he, what was he doing now at the ridge, at his post? Had he not said he could not leave the base, that it was too dangerous to accompany her back to the village? And had he not given her a necklace to stop her crying and promised to see her again the in three nights' time, and commanded her to hurry? Was he now, satiated, enjoying a cigarette, this scarred son of the soil? Or sitting, with his back against a tree, simply waiting for morning to burst upon this war-torn village, the sky pregnant with bombs, the land gangrened with hate, so that he could boast to his fellow comrades about the terrible deed on the ridge?

***

At the gate of her older sister's compound, she struggled with the chains. Their dog Spark bounded up to her, squealing, thrashing his excited tail, intelligent to her pleas for silence, her hushed appeals for secrecy; licking her pleading, patting hands, aroused by the smell of her sex. Crossing the yard, she skirted the larger of the round thatched huts, the half-finished dwelling with its yawning windows – the house that would take decades to complete. Her sister's husband was a headmaster at a school a hundred kilometres away and because of the war could only visit on special weekends or during the school holidays. Martha went to the smaller hut – the girls' hut – at the edge of the clearing.

'Shupikai. Shupi. Can you hear me?'

After what felt like an eternity Shupikai opened her large, half-asleep, half-knowing, ten-year-old, I-won't-tell-on-you niece's eyes, which gleamed in the lamp light.

'Mainini Martha, are you all right? You're late.'

'Yes, yes. Shhhh. Quiet. Just hand me the bar of washing soap and the bathing pail.'

'Are you all right, Mainini Martha?'

'I'm all right. Just hand me the pail and soap and switch off the light. Did Sisi Winnie ask about me, Shupi?'

'I told her you were in here reading. She went to bed early with the baby.'

'All right. Switch off the light. I won't be long.'

***

'Who is he?'

Sisi Winnie sat on the bed, the grumpy, bullfrog anger, which Martha had known throughout her childhood, contorting her face.

The younger woman squinted dully in the bright morning light flooding in from outside. The chickens were cackling foolishly in the yard and Spark was trying to scratch the fleas off his back and squabble with the cats at the same time. From a blaring radio somewhere the eight o'clock news was on the air and a clipped female Rhodesian voice could be heard, 'Security Force Headquarters regret to announce the death of twelve more locals caught in crossfire in a contact between Security Forces and a group of terrorist insurgents near the Gokwe Office. In the same contact, fourteen terrorists were killed and over a dozen captured with a large cache of arms. The contact has been one of the most successful since the war intensified two years ago in 1975...'

Martha realised weakly that she had overslept. How blunt and inconsequential the news seemed. So remote and yet so near. Memories of the previous night assailed her. She tried to move herself: her crutch felt heavy as a mortar, her legs stiff as pestles.

Sisi Winnie gave her no respite. The older woman's presence gripped her like a vice. 'Answer me and stop your tearful nonsense at once! It's one of the comrades, isn't it? Don't think I haven't been noticing your interest in them and your movements since you came here for your holidays. You came here to study for your 'O's not to enjoy a romantic holiday. All you're expected to do is to go to the *pungwes*, take food to the comrades and wash their clothes with the other girls. Even my daughter Shupikai knows that. But you seem to think you came here to practice being married. Do you think this is how I behaved to Baba Shupikai before he married me, flaunting myself? Is this what you've been doing at boarding school – going out with men? At sixteen! Do you think the comrades are angels just because they carry guns on their backs? Can you guess how many girls they've each slept with before they arrived in this village? Do you know how many babies they've left behind? Totemless! What if he gives you an incurable disease and your womb rots? What if he makes you pregnant? Do you think he'll care? Or marry you? And what will my husband say? Do you want him to send me away, and destroy my marriage? What if the Rhodesians come and set my house on fire? What will father and mother say, and our brothers and relatives? What will they all think?' She paused to draw breath, staring angrily at the tear-stained face of her young sister. 'Who is he?' Sisi Winnie demanded again, like an interrogator at a keep office, slapping the younger woman on both sides of the face so that the girl's ears rang.

Martha could not bear it. 'It's Comrade Ponda,' she sobbed. 'I didn't want to. He forced me.'

'Ts, ts, ts, *vana*Martha,' Sisi Winnie shook her head. What do you know about Ponda? What has he done in other operational areas? What have you heard about him? Do you think anybody would have the courage to tell you?'

'What has he done?' Her voice a muffled scream.

'Now, my young sister, you'll do as I say. Pack your bags right now. I'm taking you straight to the bus stop.'

'Where can I go?'

'Go? Don't you have a home, and a father and mother? Isn't your father still a deacon at the mission school? I know that small house is always packed with visitors and that it's not easy to study there – if that's what you want to do – but you have to go, *shamwari*.'

'You can't do this, Sisi Winnie, please,' Martha whispered. 'You know the comrades' rules. Nobody can leave or enter the village without their permission. Comrade Ponda told me so himself.'

'Listen to you. Three short weeks here and you're already the expert on the rules. Is your Comrade Ponda the only voice in this war? Did this war start with him alone? Will it end with him? Haven't I played my part? Don't the comrades know that? And aren't there enough excuses in this world? Illness? Death? Emergency? Who knows? Maybe you're pregnant already and need urgent attention. Just you wait. I'll talk back to them and we'll see if they kill me. Shupikai! Shupikai!'

'Mha!' Shupi returned her yell.

'Is the baby asleep?'

'Yes, Mhamha.'

'Bring your Mainini's suitcase from my bedroom and help her pack.'

'Where is Mainini Martha going, Mhamha?'

'Just do as I say, Shupi, and if you care for us, you'll not say a word about this to anybody, okay? Not a word, you hear!'

Shupikai slowly nodded.

***

At the front of the crowded bus an old man and a woman were humming an ancient dirge, their wizened heads bowed in unison as if to help the bus along. The heavy vehicle swerved from side to side, to avoid the landmines, people said. Martha gripped the metal bar of the back of the seat in front of her and every so often broke into tears, till the young mother beside her, wearing a white Apostolic

5

doek and nestling an infant, softly inquired, 'Is everything okay where you're coming from, *mwana wa*Mai *vangu*? Have you lost someone, a relative, perhaps to the war?'

Martha blew her nose and shook her head. She might as well have nodded because she was thinking of Comrade Ponda all right; Comrade Ponda expecting her in two nights' time and what he would do when he heard that she'd left the village without permission and Sisi Winnie, cocky Sisi Winnie, having to explain. Hurriedly, she dried her face as a roadblock loomed in front of the bus.

'Out, out, *mabhoyi*. Out, out, kaffirs. Out with your *situpas* and down with your luggage and line up along the side of the bus.'

'Come on, *madala*. Come on, *gogo*. You're the ones with daughters cooking and washing for the terrs who're causing you this shit.'

'And you conductor, leave your purse here. We don't want you handing over your takings to the terrs at the next stop. Your boss can drive back for it and help detonate a few landmines for us along the way.'

'And you, *ambuya*, is that a terr baby you're holding? What have you got in that bag of flour? Grenades? Empty it on the ground.'

'You there, young lady, hold your ID up nicely and stop messing it up with your snot. What's your name, anyway, young whore? Martha. Martha who? Listen. You'd better stop sniffling, or we'll take you to the back of the bus and teach you how to *really* holler, right guys? Going back to school, eh? Been cooking and washing up for the terrs and sleeping with them, eh? How many of them did you sleep with? Are you pregnant? Let's feel you.'

Black soldiers in their twenties and thirties in neat camouflage uniforms with shiny shaved faces, crisp military cuts and corned-beef sneers shamelessly abusing and ransacking their own people; and always, always a young white recruit, a raw school leaver, supervising, in the background, calmly smoking, as he pretended to be a man.

***

Back at school, cut off from her friends by her experience about which she could not speak, she withdrew into herself. After lights out, the dormitory often came alive with the young girls' dreams of their heroes, the *vakomana*, their bravery, their lithe strong bodies, the epitome of manhood, warriors who could rub secret lotions into their skin to enable them to evade bombs, or even disappear at will. Martha listened from afar. The bruising on her body had healed but her mind had yet to make sense of the night on the ridge, its fears and its consequences.

One night, her friend Jenet had teased her, 'What's up Martha, so quiet now you're back from the rurals. You must have fallen in love,' and she giggled. Martha heard her from faraway, a landscape of dream and romance that she had left behind.

He had taken her, partaken of her flesh, staked a claim on her soul and she could neither betray nor forget him. But the ideal that was marriage, the saccharine dreams of her friends, had left her feeling stripped, naked and there was no one to turn to for comfort or advice. To make matters worse she knew she was pregnant, and anxiety clothed her like an old dress that she daren't take off to mend or wash for fear of revealing her nudity. Around her she heard a hive of little tongues murmuring her secret to the world. Would she flunk her examinations? What would she do? What could she do? Shame, doubt, confusion, and anxiety competed for her attention.

There was no one to turn to, and fortunately no one really paid much attention, the war being a great distraction, and so her mind returned to Comrade Pondo, the man who was responsible for her condition, her desperation, and sometimes she found comfort in the idea that if only he knew that she carried his child, he would marry her. And then she would wonder who he really was? What was his name? Where did he come from? What school had he gone to? Would his family accept her? And reality would return with its harsh cold light: what would her family do if they knew she was pregnant?

Weeks dragged by and she sat for her final O-level exams. She knew she would not do as well as she'd hoped: she had not been able to concentrate to study. Failure, it seemed, fed upon itself. She saw sneers, questions, accusations on every face, even those of her best friends, and she prayed, 'Oh god, let the baby die. Let me be myself again.' But she knew that if God answered her prayers, she would feel like a murderer, and her mind twisted and turned like a trapped animal beneath her seemingly placid exterior.

When schools closed she went back to her parents' little house at the mission school. Her mother was pleased to have an extra pair of hands, noticing only that her daughter seemed much quieter and that she had put on a little weight, no bad thing in these lean war years.

Two days after she arrived home, a telegram arrived from her sister, Sisi Winnie. Come soon. Urgent. Martha was filled with trepidation but her parents did not ask too many questions, assuming her sister needed help with the baby or the housework. Her mother sighed, 'We all need you, Martha. I was counting on your help with the Mother's Union, now I shall have to manage without you. Your sister needs you more than I do.' Cautioning her at length to take care, they gave her the bus fare for the trip and the intervening twelve weeks seemed to vanish with the smell of exhaust fumes and dust.

***

'Comrade Ponda sent for you,' Sisi Winnie says again.

Ants raid the sugar in the cheap metal bowl on the creaking table and march in a steady trail to a nest somewhere in the cracked cement wall. Occasionally, Sisi Winnie takes a swipe at the table with her fat hand to clear it of bread crumbs, insects and drops of cheap red Sun jam; then she blows the remains off her fingers, wiping her plain wedding ring on the sleeve of her dress.

Martha sits opposite her sister, with her elbows on the table, her hands behind her head, studying the grain of the wood. Her suitcase stands unpacked at the side of her sister's huge Fantasy bed. Shupikai is outside pushing the baby in a pram, under a mango tree. The baby is giggling merrily – Shupi is perhaps tickling its ribs. In the yard, Spark barks forlornly and shakes the fleas off his back, wondering what to do next, too tired to pick a fight with the two black cats leaping in and out of the yawning windows of the still unfinished main house.

Sisi Winnie's husband, Babamukuru Baba Shupikai is expected tomorrow, after he has finished annotating and signing piles of smudged school reports and conducting the year-end meeting with the teachers and wondering if the school will reopen next year, and if

8

there is any point in making children go to school, and locking up the classrooms and the staff room and reminding the caretaker to water the garden and keep out intruders and checking the oil, the spark plugs, the brake fluid and the tyre pressure of his tiny Mazda pick-up truck, which he won't drive in a tearing hurry because every twenty kilometres or so he will have to stop to find out from the *mujhibhas* or *chimbwidos* if the roads are clear of mines and it's safe to proceed. And besides, he has to buy the things he promised for the comrades: cigarettes, corned beef and several pairs of jeans. And he'll have to know how to explain these if he runs into the Rhodie troops.

'Drink your tea, now, or it will get cold, Martha,' says Sisi Winnie. 'What did you eat on the bus? Did you have many roadblocks?'

Martha says little. She has almost lost her voice. She speaks with a slur that even her ears cannot pick up. She cannot speak for herself because she knows not what to think or say. Over the last three or four months she has had no control of things happening to her, or not. She has been a pawn in the scheme of things, be it the country, the land, or this war. Her young petals have unfurled in the midday heat of war and droop now waiting for the cool of the night and the reviving touch of dew. Yet her stem is firmly rooted in the soil of her quiet conviction and will not wilt.

The day is promising to be sultry, threatening to rain. It has been raining here, as elsewhere, for days. It has rained as if the skies have conspired to wash away all the blood, death and tension and clothe the world in flowers and foliage – the very camouflage that enables the comrades to strike successfully at their foe.

'I'm sorry I roughed you up, Martha,' Sisi Winnie begins again. 'There are things you could not understand, things you will never understand. Things were not what they seemed. After you left we saw fires here, *moto chaiwo*. The comrades were demanding to know where you were and why you left without permission. Comrade Ponda was furious and wanted me shot. Comrade Shu-Shine, the commander, saved me. Comrade Ponda was a dedicated fighter, but he was a very cruel man. We had all known of his ruthlessness in the areas in which he operated. If he suspected you of being a traitor, or a witch, then you

9

were done for. He'd shoot you straight in the head. The other members of his group could not restrain him. His commander wanted to send him back to Mozambique for disciplinary procedures. This was just after you had left to go back to school, Martha.

'Then there was a contact on the ridge and four comrades in Ponda's group were killed. Five Rhodesians died. An army truck was blown up. The Rhodesians took their dead away and we buried the comrades. The commander of the group called a meeting to determine who had sold out to the Rhodies. A woman was accused. A middle-aged woman, famous for growing sunflowers, married with three sons. Perhaps you have seen her large fields on the way to the bus stop. This woman was accused of spying. She had been warned many times. But nobody had proof that she was a sell-out. Perhaps people were simply jealous of her because she was a successful farmer. At the meeting, Comrade Ponda questioned her repeatedly but she wouldn't speak. Then, without warning, Comrade Ponda shot her in the head. Her blood splattered all over the gathering. The woman's husband tried to escape. Ponda shot him too. And her three sons. All in the head. One whole family wiped out, just like that. On the spot. The meeting disbanded. Villagers scurried to their houses in fear. The comrades did not try to stop them. Then, they too left hurriedly, in shame. How could they stay?

'Before they could cross the river, Ponda took ill. He became violent. His comrades took away his gun. He started shouting. His words were confused, and seemed to make no sense, but we could all hear your name. "Martha! Martha!" The village elders were called. A famous traditional healer was summoned. The healer gave him some medicine. It quieted him a little.

'He wouldn't eat. He drank only water. He wouldn't sleep. During the day he was silent as a stone, but at night he would talk like a man possessed, on and on, as if fighting his demons, and he would sometimes whisper your name, "Martha! Martha!" I heard it with my own ears. The healer and the elders asked me to send for you. They thought the sight of you might bring him back to his senses. I tried to put them off. They insisted. I asked Baba Shupikai and he said maybe we should send for you.

'Comrade Ponda is in a cave on the ridge – they call it his 'post' – guarded by one comrade and attended by the healer. Nobody else visits him.

'You won't know him,' Sisi Winnie says.

***

In the gathering dusk Sisi Winnie and Martha wait on the ridge. Martha knows the spot only too well; she vividly remembers what took place there months ago. Sisi Winnie is holding her hand.

Martha slips the necklace round her neck. She hopes that it was not once the property of some dead woman. She strokes her belly gently and steps forward.

Two men, one young, in a green cap and denims with a gun on his back, and another, elderly, stooped, a leopard skin draped over his shoulders, step out from behind the rock, leading an emaciated creature on a leash – dog or man or beardless goat – dawdling on all fours, cropping the grass and foliage sprouting in the stone crevices.

The figures approach slowly, closer now, closer, and the creature on all fours – man now, man without shirt or shoes, man in torn pants secured to wasting body with strips of bark, boy-man, raises his, its bobbing head and glances with sunken eyes at the two women. The creature turns its face slowly away, without a flicker of recognition, to munch thinly at the crop of rich green grass.

Martha cuts the scream welling inside her chest and strokes her belly.

Why Not?

On the small plane to Mbabane, Swaziland, Mercy and I sat next to each other towards the rear. In the late eighties smoking was still allowed in restricted areas of the Air Zimbabwe flights, so she lit up as soon we hit the skies and the 'no smoking' light went off. I don't smoke, so I dutifully suffered beside her. She offered me a lollipop, and as she unzipped her deep red purse to extract it, I saw a fold of new German marks, which she'd managed to smuggle through the hawk-eyed Zimbabwean emigration officials. Due to my customary precociousness, I'd only brought a sheaf of travellers' cheques and some worthless Zim-dollars.

We chatted happily, like newly reunited siblings, about everything: schools, colleges, music, books and publishers. I suspected she was roughly my age; you couldn't quite tell from her small body, long dreadlocks and sharp features. I'd heard about her, and, of course, read her novel. Indeed, in my awkward double role as a practicing creative writer and newly installed bureaucrat (masquerading under the title of 'Education Officer') I had recommended the book as 'an astonishing debut... definitely suitable to be a 'set text'. I had wondered then what she would be like in the flesh and I was somewhat relieved to find a hint of warmth and self-doubt behind her forbiddingly cultivated British accent.

The trip had been arranged by my enterprising publishers, Ken and Ingrid, and their friend Shane, a poet and compiler of repute who ran the literature programme at a prestigious multiracial school in the mountains outside Mbabane. It was he who came to collect us from the airport. A bald jolly South African exile, Shane whistled volubly while I lugged my foolishly heavy suitcase to the exchange bureau to cash a traveller's cheque. Meantime, out of the corner of my eye, I saw Mercy furtively handing over a single note to a young man in a red cap and blue palazzo, receiving in return a generous bundle of *lilangeni*. Then, pushing her light, wheel-along bag, she joined Shane, chatting and smoking, as they waited for me.

At the school, the spare, blond-haired Afrikaans principal, Mr Van Wyk, was waiting for us with two other writers, Andrew and Chris, both very slightly 'coloured' South Africans in their early thirties. (Of course, they were black, with inevitable roots in Soweto, and today they would kill me for sticking this deplorable label on them; but such were the finicky tentacles of apartheid.) We cheerily greeted each other, sizing one another up, all anxious to have a good time together. With the zeal of a schoolmaster, Mr Van Wyk at once launched into the boarding arrangements and the programme. We were to eat in the dining room with the students. We men were to sleep in an empty dormitory and Mercy was to have the spare bedroom in the headmaster's house. We were required to attend all readings and discussions but, today, Saturday, we were free. Tomorrow, Sunday, there would be an informal get-together at 3 p.m. when the head boy and girl would afterwards take us on a tour of the school. The seminar proper was due to begin in earnest on Monday morning and run for three days.

'And why must I sleep in your house, Mr Van Wyk?' Mercy demanded, forthrightly. 'Isn't that sexist?'

'Sexist?' Mr Van Wyk twisted his moustache with a quiet, discerning cough. 'Oh, no, Mercy. The bedroom is for your comfort and security.'

'So who says I won't be safe with my colleagues? I've just met them and we need to talk and get to know one another.'

'Believe you me, Mercy, this is the best arrangement.'

'And where is the nearest watering hole?' Andrew asked, deflecting this little inauspicious crisis.

'You mean pub,' laughed Shane, 'There's one at the base of the hill, about twenty minutes away on foot, but you're driving, aren't you, Andie?'

Andrew nodded and calmly picked his nose with a finger and thumb.

'Just be sure to watch your intake because the police are very strict on motorists here.'

'And are we getting paid for this?' Mercy queried again. 'I always prefer to do the contracts before we begin these things.'

Mr Van Wyk coughed again and looked questioningly at the smooth-shaven Shane, 'Oh, payment. We hadn't thought about that. We paid your air-fares and I don't suppose we could...'

'And I hate boarding-school food,' said Mercy. 'If you gave us the necessary pots and pans we could cook our own meals.'

'That might be exciting,' said Chris. 'We could do it in turns.'

'Don't try your old grandma's recipes on us, now, Chris,' laughed Andrew. 'Some of us have tricky stomachs. Can you cook, Godfrey?'

'Enough to get by,' I chuckled.

'Listen to them,' Mercy affected annoyance. 'Typical MCPs who can't boil a pot of water.'

'Pigs? I'd say swine, actually. Legion's herd, probably,' said Shane, conspiratorially.

'Who's Legion?'

'You ought to read the Good Book more often, Merç or is it Mess? Are you a mess? You don't look like one!'

'Legion is this poor tortured fellow who had a thousand evil viruses downloaded into a herd of unsuspecting porkers...'

'And these poor pigs crashed...'

'Over a cliff.'

'For which reason, Moslems and many goody-goody Christians consider pork unclean.'

'The meals are quite nice here,' Mr Van Wyk said. 'You might actually enjoy them. We don't serve pork but we try to provide variety.'

After a lunch of bream fillet and sugar beans, which tasted more like bean paste, we dumped our bags in the dorm storeroom and drove down in Andrew's hardy 504 to check out the pub. It was an old renovated house at the bottom of a hill. We lazed in bamboo chairs on the lawn in the shade of the trees. Chris ordered the first round of drinks, but Mercy insisted on paying separately for her glass of wine.

'I suggest we have a little kitty for the drinks,' she said.

Chris downed half his beer and said, 'What's a kitty?'

'Something with a little pussy, I guess,' Andrew chuckled.

'EXCUSE ME!' Mercy protested. 'We all consume different drinks, and drink at different speeds.'

Chris downed the remainder of his beer, quipping 'Hear, hear, the kitten mews.'

'Mind your language, guys.' I said. 'There's a lady here.'

'Woman, not lady, thank you,' Mercy frowned.

'What's the difference?' Andrew asked.

'Do you work for the censorship board, then, Godfrey?'

Chris and Andrew gave, or tried to give, Mercy a rough time. They enjoyed it. They mocked her British accent, and at what they perceived as her coy mannerisms and feminist convictions. At first she half relished the attention and then slowly began to take bemused offence.

'I'd say all women need a good lay,' said Chris, bluntly, downing his third beer.

'Even the Queen of England,' Andrew piped in.

'And writers too.'

'Feminist writers especially.'

'Is that all you guys can think about?' Mercy sipped her wine sparingly. 'Well, if you were thinking of going to bed with me, forget it.'

'So what kind of writer would you call yourself, Ms Mess? Africanist, Marxist, feminist, post-post-post-modernist, positivist or merely disguised traditionalist?'

'I despise labels. Why don't you read my books?'

'So you're already published then?'

'What do you think? My goodness, Chris! You say you're a well-known poet and you don't know I'm published. Why do you think I'm here, then?'

'Have you read my poetry?'

'Why should I? And I haven't come across it.'

'Hold it, hold it guys,' Andrew intervened. 'How about going dancing tonight?'

'Not with you wolves!'

'The Three Bad Wolves and the Little Virgin. We could turn it into an opera. With your valorous countryman Sir Godfrey Whatnot in attendance you'll come to no harm. Will you come with us, Godfrey?'

I looked at Mercy and her face softened as she waved her hand vaguely towards me. 'You go with them if you want to. I'm really tired and I've a page that I was writing which I want to clean up.'

'Conscientious scribe!'

'Oh, Mess's not a good sport; Mess's not a good sport.'

'We could see the place, drink, dance and relax. You can never appreciate the spirit of a place until you go to the clubs.'

'Don't say we didn't offer our services, Mess. I'll make the offer just once more…'

'Going now, going, GONE!'

'I say why don't we braai some meat?' suggested Chris, beckoning the waiter.

'Yes, why not?' said Andrew.

'No, thanks,' Mercy chirped. 'I'm full.'

'Is that why you're so skinny?'

'I like myself this way. And *stop* harassing me, you fat slob.'

'I'm not having Mr Van Wyk's dainty little six o'clock suppers. And you Godfrey?'

'I'm game.'

The waiter brought out a huge tray of fresh chicken, beef and pork cuts, and sausages. Without consulting anyone, Andrew selected a mix of portions for us and had them spiced and heaped on a platter to be taken away and barbecued.

'Yuk! I'd better go and leave you gluttons to your greasy feast,' said Mercy. 'I don't eat meat, anyway.'

'This is meat country.'

'Meat, beer and woman country.'

'Don't tell us you are veg-eat-arian.'

'Oh, Mess's a little arian; Oh Mess's a little arian.' Mercy disdainfully counted out some money onto the table.

'What on earth's that for?' asked Chris.

'For my wine and cigarettes, sir.'

'But you and Godfrey are our guests.'

'Who says? I'm nobody's guest. Guest yourself.'

'Why are you always counting money? Shove it for a present for your baby. Do you have a baby yet, Mess?'

'Why would you want to know? You want to donate one?'

'Any time.'

'Save your skimmed stuff for the sperm banks.'

'Do you want a ride?'

'He means back to the school.'

'No. I'll walk. I need the exercise.'

She picked up her bag and swung back up the hill. Her black T-shirt and Levy jeans hugging her tiny body, like a wingless insect silhouetted against the sun.

'Funny person, your countrywoman,' said Chris, when she was out of earshot. 'Was she raised in lily-white Britain or in pitch dark Zim? Are there many black women like her in Zim? Do you and she meet often?'

'No. It's my first time to meet her.'

'Are you getting along?'

'Sort of.'

Somehow I wanted to defend Mercy against their frivolous mannish onslaught, which disguised, I thought, a deeper chauvinism. I thought there was more to Mercy than they realised. I wished they had read her novel, which, though written in flawless English English, was firmly rooted in an African context. I wished they were more open to talent from the 'north'. But I also wanted to reprimand my colleague for her haughtiness. Nonetheless, my reservations aside, I was enjoying the verbal fencing.

After Mercy left we drank, ate and talked animatedly, our tongues loosened in male conviviality. Time flew and several hours later, we finally set out to look for entertainment.

'Let's go to the Why Not?' said Chris.

'Yeah, why not?'

***

The Why Not? was like a large factory warehouse. A car park, the size of two football fields, was already nearly full of an assortment of newish cars, most of which had South African number plates. Andrew, despite his obvious inebriation, proved a cautious driver and found an empty bay near the exit, and we locked up and swaggered in.

'This is where droves of white South African men unleash their fantasies upon black women,' Andrew explained with sudden bitter seriousness above the din of Michael Jackson's 'Billy Jean'. 'Under apartheid, racial mixing in sex and marriage is illegal, but the system has always found outlets for the undercurrents of its suppressed desires. Here, across the border in Swaziland, safe from the scrutiny of their wives and children, these men come to commit sin with women of colour whom they wouldn't publicly associate with at home. And, believe it or not, they take some of these women back home disguised as maids, or what not.'

'This is their Sodom and Gomorrah,' said Chris.

'Is it safe?' I asked.

'Safe as mothers.'

The place was crowded, mostly with black women, while white and black men sat and chatted over drinks in dark nooks or danced slowly on the four half-lit stages. There were also a handful of white women, a few of whom were attached to black men. I ordered a round of beers. Chris slid two fifty rand notes into my shirt pocket and said, 'Here, Godfrey. Welcome to Swaziland. We want you to have all the fun you like, you fucking Zimbo.'

'Thanks,' I said, only half embarrassed.

After a few songs, I spotted a young woman sitting quietly at an empty table and moved towards her. 'Can I join you?' She nodded and I pulled out a chair and sat down. She was about twenty-one, slightly heavy with a soft dark unquestioning face, a well-groomed natural perm, and a fluorescent beige dress. Almost every other woman in the bar was in jeans. She was not drinking, so I gallantly said, 'Can I buy

18

you a beer?' She replied, in slow, faltering English, 'I don't drinks beer.'

'What can I get you, then?'

'Coke.'

'What's your name?'

'Zanele.'

'That's a pretty name.'

I beckoned a waitress and ordered a Coke and a beer.

Chris winked and gave me the thumbs up. He and Andrew were chatting to two 'coloured' girls at a nearby table.

'Why are you in a club if you don't drink?' I challenged my new companion, just to get her talking.

'My church don't allow it,' she smiled. She had lovely white teeth.

'You have a church?'

'Yes.'

'Why are you in a club if you go to church?'

'To pass by the time. Is boring at home.'

'Do you come here often?'

'Is my second time.'

'How did you get here?'

'I hitch hikes.'

'And how will you get back home?'

'I sees later.'

'Do you live far away from here?'

'Not too much.'

I felt foolish, boyishly barraging her with questions and, as usual, offering very little about myself. But she scarcely asked me and I secretly preferred it that way. I introduced the topic of the famous annual Reed Dance ceremony in which the Swazi prince chooses a new wife from tens of thousands of nubile, bare-breasted, virgin hopefuls and she fingered the mouth of her Coke bottle with a nail and said, half admonishingly, 'Is just our custom.'

'Have you ever taken part in it?' I asked.

'Me, no. I'm too olds. And beside, me likes to have my husband to meself.'

'Are you married?'

'No.'

'Do you have a baby?'

'Me, no.'

'But how does a man handle twenty, thirty or forty wives and still try to govern a country?'

'I don't knows. Is up to the king,' she sipped her drink slowly, blinking her eyes rapidly with increasing admonition. 'Is just our custom.'

At the other table, I saw two burly white men with black sunglasses appear from nowhere, tap Andrew on the shoulder, haul him up by the collar and drag him to the toilet. Chris protested and they wagged their fingers at him and shoved him out of the way. It all happened so fast that nobody noticed, or perhaps nobody wanted to notice. The two 'coloured' girls at the table stayed put and continued smoking and drinking. I said to Zanele, 'Wait! I'll be back.' I sped over to their table. 'What's the matter?'

'Keep out of this, man!' The girls shrugged, blowing mushrooms of smoke over their drinks.

I cautiously approached the toilet by a long passage. Behind the thin wooden walls, I heard the noise of a struggle, the thump and thud of quick rough blows landing and the 'ahs' and 'ohs' of pain. Then the toilet door burst open and the two white men stormed out, flexing their wrists and blowing on their raw, red knuckles. Barely looking at me with their puffy eyes, they returned to the table and made for the exit, the two 'coloured' girls in tow.

In the toilet, Andrew was leaning over the basin, bleeding heavily from the nose and mouth. Chris was holding a roll of tissue paper out to him. 'Are you all right, Andie?' I asked pointlessly. He coughed, and blood spattered across the whitewashed wall.

'Apartheid blood,' he muttered, rinsing his fingers in the sink.

'Shouldn't we call the police?'

Andrew waved a crimson hand at me, 'No use. Those guys *are* the police. Secret apartheid agents.'

'But why would they beat you up like this, in another country?'

'You don't understand, Godfrey,' said Chris, offering his comrade more tissue paper. 'They're everywhere. They're after us all the time.'

'Especially me. The magazine I publish...'

'Those two girls you were chatting with left with the two men.'

'Probably they're spies. You never know who's who here. You're sure they've left?'

I nodded. I felt sorry for my new comrades. They now seemed so vulnerable; Chris unrolling a toilet roll, Andrew pulped up, leaning over a bloodied sink in a toilet, his manhood unraveled.

'Do you need to see a doctor?'

'Doctor, no.'

'Maybe we should get back to the dorm.'

'No, I'll be all right,' Andrew said half heroically, tidying up his face. 'We've lived with this all our lives. We don't have long to wait now. Imagine!'

'Here,' Chris offered me another note, 'Buy yourself and your missus another round and come back if you need more. Nice chick you have yourself there, comrade. Take your time, and just tell us when you want to go.'

I felt like a real sponge accepting their money but only half-heartedly tried to decline. I rationalised that some people only feel good about themselves by giving money to others, and take offence when their generosity is refused. I asked myself if his generosity was genuine. Where did his money come from? Perhaps he had a full-time job or a business? Family interests? But still somehow he made me feel guilty about my relatively well-to-do status in life. Would I offer money to a visitor to Zimbabwe?

I went back to Zanele and she asked, 'Do you knows those two coloured guys?'

I nodded, 'We came together.'

'Coloured mens' troubles. They shouldn't talks with coloured girls,' she said vaguely. 'Coloured girls for white mens. Those two white mens sits and buys the coloured girls drinks before you and your friends comes in.'

As she spoke, she slowly awakened some half-truth sleeping inside me. I sat chatting with her and began to feel very tipsy. We talked animatedly about many things, some of which I wouldn't remember. It was getting towards two o'clock and the place was still filling up. I bought a round of drinks for Andie and Chris. Zanele slowly sipped her second Coke. When it was nearly finished, she said, 'I think I goes now. Tomorrow morn I gets up early.'

'How will you go?'

'I go outside and sees.'

'My friends and I will take you home,' I offered recklessly.

'You have car?'

'My friends do. Wait. I'll ask them.'

Chris said, yes, we could take her home, and Andrew laughed, 'Of course, why not?' They downed their drinks and we went in search of our car in the cemetery of metal. Chris drove and Andy reclined in the front passenger seat. I cuddled in the back with my head on Zanele's lap. She gave Chris directions. Andrew reached out a hand over the seat and fondled my head and Zanele's knees.

'I want you to be good to our friend, Zanele. Real good, you know,' Chris chortled

He drove very fast, swerving round corners on the narrow dirt twin-track. Darkened buildings and forlorn lights leapt out of nowhere and flew past. He cut into the crop of tall grass and missed a dead tree trunk. The car coughed, grunted and whined. Andrew muttered, 'Shit, Chris! Shit man!' He reached out and fondled us again, stroked my face and the inside of Zanele's thighs. I could smell soap and a slight perfume off Zanele's body. She sat still, cradling my head in her hands and shrinking back slightly as if nothing less than this was to be expected from a cohort of drunken men. After what seemed like a long time we broke into a bright scatter of lights, ploughing on till Zanele said, 'There, there. The next one. This house. Here. Stop.'

I don't recall how we got out of the car or into Zanele's room but in the roar of pounding waves between my ears I vaguely remember her soft dark face half smiling, and in the pale light, Zanele looming down on the edge of the mattress and Andrew falling or crouching down and stroking my neck and Zanele's face, whispering, 'Good now, be good now both of you,' and Chris hooting outside and me sliding into rattling snores and suddenly Chris banging on the door and calling out our names, and shaking us up, and snapping me out of myself, Chris pleading, 'Come now, Andie, let's go; okay Godfrey, you can stay, we'll come back for you in the morning, right?' And Andrew staggering towards the door and me curling up towards Zanele on the bed...

***

Hours later, I woke up. The afternoon sun blazed through the thin blue cotton curtains. I was alone on the bed in my T-shirt, my jeans abandoned on the floor. Zanele was not there. I groggily croaked her name but there was no answer. I looked at my watch. It was two o'clock. At one end of the room was a doorway covered by a yellow plastic curtain. I called again but there was no reply. Staggering onto my feet, I pulled at the curtain and blinked into the bathroom – she wasn't there. A sudden panic gripped me: had she had locked me in? I tried the door. It was mercifully open. I riffled through my pockets and purse; all my money and IDs were safe.

I sank again onto the soft mattress and thought, 'Oh, the programme! Mr Van Wyk's get-together at three and the tour of the school afterwards! Would I be able to make it? And where was I? Where was Zanele? Why hadn't Chris and Andy come back for me? Had they forgotten or got lost on the way? And what was Mercy doing? And Shane?'

I explored the room. Rectangular, with a low mud ceiling, it was furnished with a three-quarter bed and two small green plastic sofas. On the floor there was a low stool covered with Zanele's toiletries, and an open suitcase full of clothes, some pressed and folded, others creased from recent wearing. On a shelf stood a primus stove, a few pots and plates and a bunch of religious tracts from the Watch Tower church. There were two empty quart bottles, some loose change and a message in a surprisingly neat scrawl: *Coming soon beer and meats at corner's street.* The window opened out onto a small, parched garden; the beige dress she'd worn the night before was fluttering on the sagging clothesline, newly washed, but there appeared to be the remains of a round brown stain at the waist. I opened the door and looked down the street. The houses were haphazardly built and all at different stages of completion. Some were mud brick shells, a few had a strata of fired bricks brazenly embedded in cement, others had roofs of corrugated zinc sheets weighted down by large rocks and stout blocks of wood. One or two of the finer buildings carried satellite dishes on the roofs. There were people on the dusty streets and a half recognisable dialect trickled through gaping windows.

I took a shower and the rope of cold water from the mangled faucet helped beat out my dazedness. As I was rubbing her lotion onto my skin I noticed drops of blood on the white pillows. I pulled down the bedding and discovered more blood on the sheets. My heart sank, fear and doubt in the well of my stomach. What had happened? Was I safe? God, please no! My mind was clouded with conflicting emotions. I couldn't wait for Zanele to return.

She returned after three, and in the light of the day in her white, sleeveless Sunday dress and flat pink shoes she seemed younger and slimmer than I'd imagined. She said, 'When did you waking up? I leaving some monies for you for meats and beer. Has your friends comes yet?'

'No. Maybe they forgot. I was waiting for you. I didn't know where to go. And besides, I couldn't leave your door unlocked.'

'Is no problem. Nobody opening other doors here. People no steal here.'

'Where were you?'

'I teaches crèche children. Todays was Sunday school. We having birthday part for one childs.'

'Really?'

'Me tells you this morning. I tries wakes you up and you just "hm, hm".'

'Now how do I get back to the school?'

'There's bus at five o'clocks. I goes buy you some foods and cooks for you. Okay?'

She took the money and the empty quarts from the shelf, went out momentarily and returned with meat, vegetables and beer. As she cooked, I drank a quart and felt better. After we'd eaten, I mustered the courage to ask her about the stains on the pillows and the sheets.

'Oh, bloods,' she said, shaking her head resignedly. 'Your coloured friend coughing and blowing nose and I says to him, "Go now go" and he cough coughing cough blood till other one comes takes him to car.'

'And me?'

'You sleeps flats out whole night.'

'Why didn't you send me out to the car too?'

'Becos I sees you are drunkend and I says he my friend and talking to me nice all night so let her rest small small.'

'So we didn't...'

'I don't sleeps with mens,' she said, candidly. 'Young womans here don't sleeps with mens becos of Reed Dance. Is just our custom. See?'

Later, when she took me to the bus terminus, she asked me if I would come again and I promised to try to do so next evening, even though I knew it was unlikely. I would have been happy to return. I felt as if I had known the young woman for ages. I took down her address and promised to write or to look her up if I ever returned to Swaziland. When I offered her the hundred rand which Chris had given me, and fifty more of my own, she smiled and said, 'All this?' and I said, 'Yes, take it' and she said, 'You ares very kind,' and I said, 'You too.'

I stumbled onto the crowded bus, found a seat and waved to her. She waved back before turning down the dusty street.

***

At the swish mountain school, the news had spread that Chris, Andrew and I had got hopelessly drunk at a sordid down-town club, provoked a fracas over some women, got severely beaten up (Andrew thrashed almost lifeless, Chris's tongue sliced out and my spine broken); that despite our injuries we had raced into the night carrying off one prize woman – mine – with our assailants hot on our tails, and that I was holed up somewhere in the township. Chris and Andrew had one way or another returned, the latter all bandaged up, and Chris had spent the morning driving around the township looking for me but because of his mutilated mouth he could not ask for directions and had lost his way in the unnamed streets.

All that had left Mercy alone for the informal get-together and the tour.

So when I turned up, slinking into the dorm at dusk, I was something of a ghost and everyone was first amazed, then relieved. Andrew, sitting up in bed, assured everyone that he was fine; Shane, Chris and Mercy (the latter clean, poised and perfumed) were discussing what to do about me with a dismayed Mr Van Wyk, who was considering cancelling the event. Mercy was furious and unappeased. She accused me of deserting her, of shaming us, Zimbos, of very nearly forcing her to call home and inform our publishers of this self-inflicted disaster. Shane, sympathetic and conciliatory, managed to convince Mr Van Wyk to go ahead with the seminar. I apologised profusely, realising that I had been an absolute fool to let things happen as they did and to have taken advantage of everyone around me.

In the morning the readings began with a flourish. Chris's poetry was amazing, his vivid imagery and subject matter immediately struck a chord with the young audience; my novel was well received and Andrew's critique of contemporary southern African literature (despite being delivered from an arm-chair in a low, rather monotonous voice from a bandaged mouth) was learned and impressive. Mercy's presentation very nearly stole the show: she read beautifully and had, I thought, the advantage of being the only woman on the panel.

But she was difficult throughout the short stay; she insisted on changing the programme, coming first in everything and having the lioness's share of the time. None of us minded her: Chris, Andy and Shane kept trying to humour her. She almost threatened a boycott when the promised contracts were not forthcoming and she demanded to have the students discuss her own novel and not Alice Walker's *The Color Purple*, which, she declared, 'was not worth all the fuss'. She had already complained about having to be shut up in the principal's house after eight, not being permitted to smoke in her room, and so on. So when the flustered principal asked me to talk about Alice Walker, I said, 'Why not?' put on my teacher's cap and spoke as ably as I could. Gratified, Mr Van Wyk smiled and Shane pumped my arm and said, 'Way to go, Godfrey!'

I felt I had half atoned for my misdemeanours.

After my discussion of *The Color Purple*, Mercy looked dubious.

I felt that I'd let her down and rationalised that perhaps she would never grasp the paradoxical richness of adversity that I as an artist had experienced, and knew I would make use of one day.

Queues

Some time in the early prime of my life I lost faith in myself.

In the mid-seventies Sisi Elizabeth earned twenty-two dollars a month working for white people. I hauled my trunk, black like a coffin and heavy with books, into her little wooden cabin at the back of that hideously large yard. I arrived bruised and sore, expelled from school, utterly desperate, banished for raising my tender adolescent fists against Rhodesia. Sisi Elizabeth returned every now and then from the white mansion and wiped her creased brow with her apron and adjusted her nanny's cap and said, 'But cousin, you must be starving. What will you have to eat? Don't be afraid, they are not here. They are away on holiday in Cape Town. Monkey Valley or something.' I shoved my modesty into my shorts and she took me to the house and showed me a 'dick freeze' loaded to the neck with steaks. I reclined in a resplendent lounge, timidly sampling Dolly Parton records and *Illustrated Life* and *Personality* magazines in that strange superior house. Later I gorged myself on the spaghetti and mince and cheese she had prepared. For a week while I waited for the news of this latest disaster to get through to my parents, I lived in that white house, eating rich strangers' food, listening to rich strangers' records and writing angry stories on a strange typewriter.

Rudo said I had to believe in myself. Expulsion sometimes felt like a bad start.

I was on the plane fleeing from I know not what going to I know not where and I know not why. I saw her profile and black-stockinged legs and short hair and the rings on her fingers and I recognised her at once. University. A quarter of a century ago. Sociology or Law. Probably now some NGO chef. She was dozing, her face turned up to the ceiling of the plane, perhaps meditating in the peaceful way people do when they are flying among the clouds, miles above the world. I mastered the courage to accost her. She spoke to me with the quick shallow warmth and precocious airs of women who become widows too early in life, of women who clutch at the tattered shreds of perceived bliss, of single mothers who cling to files and reports and Bibles to bolster their waning sanity in a vicious world. She baffled me with her newly acquired strength. I tried to be level with her, to hide the horns of my chauvinism. I tried to be honest and serious with her, with myself; not to flirt; not to patronise or to be frivolous; to avoid shocking her with the depth of my depression. She said earnestly, 'Call me any time and we can talk. But don't you have a wife to love?'

Once upon a time in the days of Sisi Elizabeth a loaf of bread cost twelve cents and you could buy a kilogram of meat for a dollar. Twice upon a moon your father sent you, by registered mail, two dollars pocket money to last half a term. Thrice upon a star you ate chicken and chips for twenty-five cents, and with Sidney at the end of the term you patrolled the train at night, munching five-penny mints and Choice Assorted biscuits. Four times upon a sun your father sent three siblings to boarding school on a milkman's pay. Five times upon a galaxy you had rice and chicken for Christmas. Six times upon the universe you were poor, but you survived.

The rains came. Rivers gurgled and dams burst, but not all the time. Hippos waded out of the rich mud. The spirits of the land smiled, and sometimes frowned. Without fertilisers you could reap thirty bags of maize and thirty-five bags of groundnuts from ten acres and the GMB sent you back with your unwanted produce, or with peanuts in your pockets. If you reaped nothing you pawned a beast for a bag of grain.

You were dirt poor, but you seldom starved.

I told Rudo that I wanted to believe in myself.

I told her I wanted a good woman to help me do that, that the best thing for a man was a good woman. A good, funny, honest woman. A woman to enjoy, to like, to love, to talk to, to laugh with, to devour, to feast on. A soul- and brain-mate. A woman who does not take herself too seriously and does not do too much of the church stuff. An intelligent woman who knows what she's about and has many layers to her that I can slowly peel off. A woman who is dependable, yet will allow me the foolishest of my fantasies. A woman who will help me organise myself. A woman who will let me talk to Hazvina or Memory or Nontokozo, and will not imprison my imagination.

'You must be an aspiring polygamist, then,' laughed Rudo.

'I suspect so,' I replied. 'My grandfather had two.'

'And what became of him and his wives? Did he become another statistic in a classic case of poisoning?'

'Okay, things did not work out well. They never do, but polygamy could be beautiful. If I had two wives we would live and love and laugh together, dress to kill and go out as a threesome.'

'Where would you find women like that?'

'They must be there somewhere in this universe.'

'You, an educated man, saying such things. The feminists will immolate you.'

'I hope not.'

'Do you see a woman merely as an object?'

'God, please no.'

'Okay – but why do you want to be mothered so much? Why do you want to define yourself in terms of another person?' Why why why?

In '67 and '73 there was drought, but that was before independence. Our mothers served us yellow sadza on the tables – the infamous 'Kenya' – so called because some of that brand of maize was imported from East Africa. In 1980, the year of our independence, Chaminuka and Nehanda smiled and released a deluge of rain to wash away all the blood and pain of the war. Crops flourished. Livestock lowed and baa-ed and bleated joyously in the plains, munching luscious grass. Even the backyards of township houses and the scrapland between factories and townships boasted greenly of abundant harvests. Silos filled fatly, trains thundered thankfully away to foreign lands, laden with exports. We were given sweet reprieve. We were declared the bread-basket of the region.

I met Rudo for lunch a few weeks after we got back home. She had on a black see-through blouse and an ankle-length denim skirt with a long slit on the side. She wore lipstick and a dark eye-shadow; her short hair had a special glow. I could tell she had done something to make herself look OK. She possessed a quiet simplicity that made me ache longingly within, that made me gasp at the degree of my despair, at the extent of my famine. She drank mineral water and ordered a cheese and tomato sandwich, which she carefully nibbled. She staunchly refused to take wine or spirits or beer, saying that she drank only on very special occasions and when she didn't have to go to work, saying that her late husband had only persuaded her to take the occasional glass. I sombrely sipped my beer and fingered the bank notes in my pocket and tried to be engaging. Her answers were short. She seemed to be hovering on the borders of her own dilemma, waiting for some decided declaration from me. She laughed briefly and politely at my jokes, judging me, trying to fathom the reasons and nature of my interest in her. I wondered if she was worth the effort, if she was not chained too much to propriety; why I needed to be with her, why she readily let me pay the bill, what it would take to make her unshackle herself from herself.

We declared independence, after that long bitter war, in 1980. In the late eighties we tried to unshackle ourselves from the past. Out went the chains of the old constitution and in came the new. Out went the premiership and in came the presidency. We ploughed forward with a show of fisted arms, with calls for reconciliation, a brave new unity and work. Of course, there weren't enough funds. It wasn't easy. We massacred each other. We manufactured enemies. We squandered resources. There was mistrust, gangrene setting in. There were die-hards who chose to shit in the face of forgiveness. We fumbled with propriety, with new challenges. The world was watching, avariciously. We invited the world out for dinner and she coyly agreed. The world came with a wig and sweet-smelling musk, large round earrings, a black T-shirt, a short denim skirt and black *gogo* shoes. She was bra-less and pant-less and we leapt to her, our mouths drooling. The world ordered a rock shandy and a tuna-fish sandwich and watched us while we knocked back lager after lager and gorged ourselves on sadza and cows' hooves. The world watched as we paid the bill, then she gave the waiter a little tip.

Rudo wanted me. She wanted to win me over bit by bit. She called me day in day out. She left innumerable messages with my maid and my children asking me to call her. I think my estranged wife saw the messages. I feared for myself. I suspected that like me, Rudo wanted to believe in somebody else so that she could believe in herself, and redefine herself. I suspected she did the church stuff, however mildly, in order to belong to something. She declared she was Catholic, that she had a rabid mistrust of the new born-again churches. I didn't believe in myself and I didn't belong to anything. But I knew I could not leave her; that I had started something that I could not stop. Rudo wanted me but she really did not want me. Her sudden change of heart bothered me. She wanted me to respect myself, to help me salvage myself from what she thought was self-imposed gloom, but she wanted to own me like a toy. She even called me Teddy Bear. Teddy Bear! I felt a kind of pity for her. She lived with her eight-year-old daughter, her only child, in a two-bedroomed flat in a well-to-do block in the Avenues. The flat was cosy and tastefully furnished. I played CDs of the Beatles, Fleetwood Mac, Elton John, Joan Armatrading, Thomas Mapfumo, Miriam Makeba and Chiwoniso Maraire. She also had several gospel CDs by Mechanic Manyaruke and

Shuvai Wutawunashe, and when I ignored the latter I told her that God had eluded me, had been too hard on me and my family.

People are defined by the music they keep and play but she confused me because of the ambiguity of her choices. I suspected some of the older music had been merely left by her husband and now she was using it to bait men. She drove an old-model Mazda which, perhaps, like her, was rust-eaten but efficient. I asked if some of her property had been left to her by her late husband, but she would not be drawn to tell me. Her daughter was beautiful and intelligent and liked me at once. Her name was Tariro. Tariro saw me like a father figure, a friend. I could tell she needed a father to cling to, somebody to love her, somebody who did not, like her mother, just order her to wash her feet or eat all her vegetables or switch off the TV and go to bed. Tariro loved books and I brought her some of the ones I had written. She curled up on the floor, between my legs, with her head in my lap and asked me to read to her. She told me the stories that she liked. She and her friends in the block decided to act out one of my children's plays. She wanted them to stage the play for me but two members of the group were away and they could not do it. When she went to bed she hugged me and kissed me on the lips and her little tongue touched mine.

Rudo smiled at me and said, 'But did you ever do this to your own children?'

I stood up guiltily and went to change the CD.

We bit off more than we could chew. We started starving bit by bit. Our teeth ached from raw meat and bone and there were not enough carcasses, not even enough dentists, so we went for the soft stuff. The national cake was getting smaller, but suddenly everyone wanted a piece. The bakeries hiccupped and coughed and sent out frantically for more wheat. The teachers wanted the cake, before it was even baked. The nurses wanted it. The doctors wanted it. The soldiers wanted it so badly that they sent in battalions in brand new Bedfords to bring it back in truckloads. The ex-combatants wanted it. The farmers wanted it. The peasants wanted it. The workers wanted it. Little children in the schools cried for milk and soup, for buns, for books. Pastors and priests in the pulpits of poverty pined for Lazarus' pitiful morsel. We squandered the national cake then turned to ordinary bread, but even that was not enough. We put up impressive schools, clinics, roads and dams. We gazetted new minimum wages, instituted quotas in workplaces, demarcated growth-points. But the new classrooms pleaded for desks, clinics squabbled for food and medicines, sun-baked roads yawned for bridges and asphalt. We printed more money. We imported doctors and teachers from other lands. We sent out planeloads of our own school-leavers to train in foreign languages, on foreign islands, so that they could come back to teach their own. We thirsted for education.

I had begun to thirst for her. She was slyly putting me through some kind of probation, as if to test me. She wanted to see whether I would behave myself and prove to be worthy of her. She deliberately called it a probation and it lasted weeks. She was clicking me off in the computer-brained folders of her psyche. I was sure she wanted me too. Perhaps it was true she had lain fallow for years, that she had survived the droughts and famines of her life, that she was now waiting dangerously to be ploughed up and seeded and fertilised. But she was holding on. Hanging in there. I felt we were both too old to pretend, that we did not need to follow any cardinal rules, that we could pass the litmus test of morality as long as we did not rob or envy or steal or maim, or do or wish anybody ill; that we could commit the lesser offences with reasonable impunity.

Our probation with the world was interminable. Night after night we took the world out for dinner and she ordered a shandy and a tuna sandwich while we knocked back lager after lager and wolfed down platefuls of cows' hooves. We would pay the bill and she would give the waiter a tip. At weekends we would order whiskies then after several glasses we became incomprehensible and had to order a taxi home. We paid the fare and the world gave the driver a tip. Later on the world would agree to go upstairs for a cup of coffee. She took off her earrings and slipped out of her *gogo* shoes and wiped off her lipstick and eye-shadow and let down her hair and perched on the edge of the bed and chirped, 'Not quite yet, not quite yet.' She counted off on her fingers our crimes and shortcomings and reproached us but we did not listen. She said, 'Stop giving ex-combatants grants,' but we did not listen. She said, 'Stop subsidising commodities,' but we did not listen. She said, 'Stop controlling prices,' but we did not listen. She said, 'Devalue your currency,' but we did not listen. She said, 'Stop tampering with the land,' but we did not listen. She said, 'Stop grabbing farms,' but we did not listen. She said, 'Okay, reimburse the white farmers you kicked out,' and we said, 'No, you do that. They are your offspring; your kind. Great-grandchildren of red-necked boys who called themselves policemen and armed themselves with rifles and rode shamelessly into our villages at dawn and planted the Union Jack and each earned themselves miles of savanna from some dainty little woman called Queen Victoria. You give us money to buy them out.' She said, 'But we've already given you the money for that,' and we said, 'Peanuts!' She said, 'You squandered that money. And there already is lots of government land lying unused,' and we said, 'Nonsense.' She said, 'But you've got to look at things differently. This is not the twentieth century any more. You can't go on flogging the colonial horse. The colonial horse is dead. You've got to find yourselves new horses, new mules. You've got to survive. You've got to change your ideas. You can't go on excusing your corruption and inexperience forever, and persecuting each other. You've got to have the rule of law.'

We were confused. We did not speak with one voice. Some of us said, 'Leave the white farmers alone,' and others said 'No way!' Some of us said, 'Don't destroy the soul of this land, the farming industry, the economy – don't turn this gem of a country into a land of peasants,' and others replied, 'Better be poor on your own land than be slaves forever.' In the towns sleek residents clicked their tongues in disapproval. In the country tottering grandmothers and grandfathers and newly reformed rustics rejoiced at the pieces of their ancestral

35

land that were restored to them, at the little seed packs, thrifty bags of fertilisers and itinerant tractors that were availed to them. In disbelief they partitioned pastureland, dairy fields and miles of tobacco. They put up little pole and dagga huts and tilled the land with cattle and donkeys and iron ploughs. Other new farmers came purely out of greed – veritable new settlers, with not an iota of the farming instinct in their veins. Some ex-combatants and chefs were among that lot. They bullied peasants out of furnished farmhouses and barns and eyed rich valleys and well developed properties the way pot-bellied, cigar-smoking, inebriated businessmen eye virgins selling snacks outside beerhalls. Aggrieved white farmers packed up and abandoned their houses and lands to seek refuge in city flats or hotels or neighbouring countries. Highways and country roads were littered with tractors, harvesters and irrigation equipment, abandoned, pillaged or lined up for sale. The borders of chiefdoms were expanded and redefined – unwary chiefs suddenly found themselves in a quandary as their chiefdoms suddenly shrank or expanded, some of their subjects dispersed and some became victims of new ever-changing laws. The world did not speak with one voice either. It quarrelled with itself. Some voices pleaded, 'Leave this little country alone,' and the most strident among the other lot shrilled, 'No, this precedent is bad for the world, a prescription for chaos and disrespect for the rule of law. This country must be stopped at all costs – punished, humiliated, isolated, starved and squeezed until it goes down on its knees and accepts defeat.'

Rudo lies on her back on top of the sheets, spent, nursing her new dilemma. Her hair is damp, her forehead laced with sweat, her eyes blank and her mouth half open. She is half facing me, with one arm thrown in wild abandonment over my chest. My heart is slowing and stilling; I am almost numb, pervaded by a deep sense of emptiness and loss. Our clothes are strewn all over the red-carpeted floor; her elegant clock clucks three on the wall. In the adjacent bedroom little Tariro coughs and moans in her sleep.

There is something ambivalent about conquests and defeats. Something innately sad.

'You never talk about your wife,' Rudo smiles, weakly.

I don't answer. Some pain is beyond words. I am stripped of all my defences. Rudo continues, 'Why don't you just divorce her if she doesn't make you happy? It's bad for you both and it's bad for your children. Many people like you suffer because they don't opt out, because they live their lives for other people, for their parents or children or neighbours and the like. Why don't you go and get yourself a hot-blooded young lass from the high density areas – the kind with O-levels who work as typists and will serve you fried lizard tails to soften up your brain?'

'Suppose I've already had one?'

'Have you? What was her name?'

'Nontokozo.'

'What was she like? What does she do?'

'Never mind. Just don't talk badly about other women. Don't look down on other women because of their class or education or whatever. Never ever ever.'

'Does it bother you so much?'

'What about you?' I croak back. 'Who are you living for?'

'Myself.'

'Are you using me?'

'No.'

'Do you want me to marry you?'

'Of course not.'

'Is it friendship you want, then?'

'Maybe.'

'Are you a feminist?'

'Maybe. Maybe not. I was never a textbook person. I never blindly believed in any "isms". And besides, who says a feminist doesn't need a good lay?'

We never truly believed in any '-isms'. We were born capitalists, raised capitalists; we lived with racism; we flirted with Marxism; we heard about humanism and *hunhuism*, we briefly espoused socialism, in lecture theatres we even dabbled with feminism and classism and ageism and now we are squashed again with the capitalists. Full circle. Perhaps the only '-isms' we truly knew were chauvinism and sexism. Maybe one day the good old world will agree to knock back several lagers and scuds and wolf down a few cows' hooves for an aphrodisiac and agree to go home with us and she will take off her earrings and rip off her wig and slip out of her *gogo* shoes and wipe off her lipstick and eye-shadow and, lo and behold, slip out of her bra-less, pant-less dress and tuck herself into bed with us and she will dream us up a brand new '-ism'. For bitter or worse, till death do us part, as Clopas Wandai J. Tichafa wrote.

Rudo and I did not part easily. Oh no, she didn't die. Not yet anyway. On the contrary, she started showing me off to her friends. She started saying, 'Let's go and see so and so.' Or, 'Let's go out with so and so.' Or she would say, 'Tariro is lonely. Why don't we take her out to meet her cousins?' She introduced me to people as her friend, which was fair enough, but there was always a question hovering over our relationship. People knew I was attached, that what I had going on with her could at best be described as an affair. But sooner or later we would have to come to terms with ourselves, with each other. She had a special friend that she liked, a beautiful nurse called Jean. Jean was pregnant, expecting a baby – her second – anytime. Jean was our age, perhaps a bit younger, and I thought she was taking a big gamble having a baby. Perhaps the baby was an accident, or she had done it willingly. She said the man had run off somewhere or other. I didn't ask. I couldn't ask. There are things you don't ask. We went out together, Rudo and Jean and I, and had drinks and she made us a delicious pot of oxtail, tripe and intestines. We listened to rumba and jazz and talked. I asked Jean if it was okay for the baby if she drank wine and she said, 'No problem. You can't live by the book all the time. After all, rules are meant to be broken.' I wanted to believe her. After all, she was a nurse. The wanted, hunted kind who were fleeing our ramshackle clinics and flocking out to the world to work in lavish, well-lit

hospitals. I liked Jean. She was a survivor. She laughed a lot,
a tinkling little laugh. She and I created a wicked camaraderie
and we fenced Rudo in with it, into our circle. She wanted
Rudo to be happy. She nursed Rudo out of her loneliness. She
had small features, a kind of quick precariousness. I knew
what she would be like once she delivered the baby. She was
going to have a Caesar. I did not ask why she was going to
have one when she looked so healthy. I couldn't ask. There are
things you don't ask. Rudo glowed with pride. She was happy
to have me, to have Jean. To have friends.

After the thorny land business, we quickly lost our friends. One by one they packed their bags and left, most without saying goodbye. We woke up in the morning and found their houses and offices empty and their doors and windows wide open. There was rubbish on the unswept floors, cracked windows in the bathrooms and some of the toilets did not flush. We wrenched out their drawers and found condoms. We flung open their cupboards and found only paper-clips and pins. We raided their kitchenettes and found remnants of mouldering meals. We rummaged through their trashcans for valuables and found useless coins. The world phoned back long-distance with a crackling voice and said, 'Look, you little truant, just say you are sorry and we will come back,' and we sulked. The world said, 'Look, we want to come back and play with you. We'll give you back your marbles and bring you many more. We'll give you liquorice and candy and cake and teddy bears,' and we sulked some more. The world said, 'Now you're going to be really sorry.'

Now we were really sorry. The banks ran dry. We queued helplessly for cash that wasn't there. The industrialists went off to visit our neighbours. We ran out of foreign exchange. Our friends said, 'Enough is enough. You are a bad friend. You don't pay your debts. Now we can't give you any more fuel. Now we can't give you any more food,' and we cried,' We'll give you half our estates – we'll mortgage them to you,' and they said, 'Okay, but that's not enough.' We ran around borrowing. Borrowing and borrowing. Borrowing from other friends. Borrowing from ourselves. We borrowed and borrowed until we borrowed the word borrow. Now we were really, really, sorry. We had no power. We had no electricity; aeons of coal lay unmined beneath our trees and rocks and mountains. Our own spirits, Chaminuka and Nehanda, sulked and turned against us. They said, 'No more rain, kids.' For years in a row we had no rain. It was the worst drought in memory. Crops wilted in the fields. Rivers ran dry. Cattle tore down the thatch off roofs and chased women carrying empty buckets. Baboons invaded households and grabbed live chickens. Animals died in the plains. We had no food to eat. Our shops were bare. Our granaries sneezed dust. We turned to Chaminuka and Nehanda and said, 'But what have we done? How can we have a drought now, when we have other problems?' Chaminuka and Nehanda sulked. Chaminuka caressed the knob of his staff and looked away from us, towards the distant hills. Nehanda picked the threads off her cloth and said, 'You know what you did.' We said, 'We don't understand. Please explain,' and she said, 'You are too young to know. One day you will know.' Now we had no water to drink. Our dams filled with sand. Our taps ran dry. We stood in queues in the scorching sun, taking turns to suck the greenish water trickling from rusty taps. We dug wells in our backyards. Our toilets leaked into our wells. We got sick. We went to empty hospitals. There were no beds. There were no medicines. There were no nurses. The nurses had run off to lavish, well-lit hospitals in foreign lands. There were a few doctors who spoke a funny language. Prices doubled every month. There were massive retrenchments. We turned to strikes, stay-aways and go-slows. We printed more and more money.

Rudo did not have much money. She had only seemed to have much money. She did not worship money, really. She was a civil servant, a poor struggling servant, a widow in her early forties, but she was content with what she had. She wanted something more than money, something she could not define, or was not prepared to define. She wanted to share her time, her miseries, herself with somebody else. She did not want my money, really. She wanted something else from me. Or so I thought. But we sometimes talked about money. Money, money, money. Like when I couldn't buy Tariro a jumbo-size pizza because the price had doubled overnight. Like when she showed me her latest salary slip with nothing on it but deductions. Like when she showed me her monthly medical-aid bills. Like when she told me she had to see three specialists every month. Like when she told me, out of the blue, out of the very, very blue, out of the bluest of blues, that she was a chronic manic-depressive. Like when she told me she had taken herself off medication because it was too expensive, and addictive. Like when she told me she had turned to yoga and meditation to get to sleep. Like when she told me she had a brain tumour for which she would have to be operated on outside the country. Like when she told me her Mazda needed a complete overhaul. Like when she showed me papers from the Salary Service Bureau detailing the paltry amounts she would get if she took an early retirement package for health reasons. Like her plans to buy a stand, or rent a stall at a flea market, or even purchase a hammer mill to grind maize if she got that precious package. Like when she asked me if we could take Jean out to comfort her after her miscarriage. I did not know how to help her. I was impotent before her wishes. If she had asked to borrow money I could have considered helping her, very much against my better instincts, I suppose, but she never asked. Not directly anyway. Perhaps the word 'borrow' did not exist in her vocabulary, or had once existed, and long ago expired. Perhaps she had already borrowed the word borrow.

Last Wednesday I was in the petrol queue all day. I phoned the garage and they told me they might have something that day and when I rushed out there I found a kilometre-long stretch of cars waiting. It was six in the morning. I was hungry and unwashed and hastily dressed. The queue snaked round three street corners and at the mouth of the garage it split into four columns of cars. The diesel queue, the trucks and kombis and buses and lorries, wound in from the opposite direction. They had camped for two days in the queue, waiting. There was pandemonium at the garage. The road was blocked. The garage attendant and security men were battling with a rush of blaring cars.

A policeman was negotiating with a ring of enraged drivers. This garage usually received petrol every day but for the past few days it had had nothing. Petrol, no diesel; diesel, no petrol. It was always like that. Alternating. If you had one then you didn't have the other. I made a U-turn and parked behind the last car in the queue. The queue was not moving. I did not go to work. It was no use going to work when you did not know if you could get there and how you would come back. Somebody in our lift club had taken my children to school and I just *had* to find the fuel to go and pick them up and bring them back. I got out of the car and talked to other men under the trees. We talked about garages that sold petrol to selected customers at night. We talked about backstreet boys who sold the stuff at ten times the official price. We talked about cars or households that had gone up in flames when unwary hoarders lit up cigarettes or candles in makeshift store rooms. We talked about ailing wives; about children who go to fancy schools and talk with funny accents and refuse to cook for their daddies; about newly elevated company directors who stashed away billions. We talked about mushrooming churches that made fortunes from unsuspecting millions. We talked about the drought. We talked about new farmers who won prizes growing wheat and winter maize. We talked about others who stole irrigation pipes and fencing wire and tried to sell them off. We talked about price freezes. We talked about hoarding. We talked about houses in the townships where one could buy, at five or six times the normal price, unlimited supplies of bread, sugar, maize, mealie-meal, salt and cooking oil without having to join the queue. We talked about queues at the banks, in the supermarkets, in the pubs, at the bus stops, at the mortuaries, at the cemeteries. We talked about people stumbling like zombies, waking up at three in the morning to get to work and getting home at midnight. People turning into alcoholics to survive each and every day. We talked about catastrophes on the highways, of smashed up designer cars, of busloads of students burnt to ashes on the roads, of overturned trucks and mangled trains; the foul breath of unappeased departed souls prowling the air. We talked about men who now deserted their wives for days and slept with their girlfriends on the pretext that they were in

42

the petrol queue. We talked about crime and divorce. We talked about AIDS.

We argued about elections.

'Our case is beyond politics,' said one resident drunk. 'We need some kind of supernatural intervention.'

The woman in the twin-cab behind me heard us and smiled and vaguely nodded us on. She threw her head back over the seat and tried to sleep. It was hot. I bought two pink freezits from a vendor and offered her one and she said 'Thank you' and sucked on it and tried to go back to sleep. I wanted to talk to her, but I don't think she had had breakfast. There were cases of cosmetics in the cab. I wondered if she was a shop owner or a sales lady. Or a border jumper.

At four o'clock Rudo phoned me on my cellphone to ask me where I was. She said she had tried to get me all day but as usual the network was jammed. She said she had not phoned me at home because I had told her not to. The other day when my phone was dead she had decided to burn up precious juice and driven right up to my gate and hooted me out to give me a brand new shirt for a Valentine present. I had reluctantly accepted it and thanked her but told her not to come to my house again. The gardener and the maid could see her. My children could see her. Besides, I didn't care a hoot for Valentine's Day and Christmas and New Year's Day and Independence Day and the like. I was too old for that. Holidays depressed me. I told her she must stop leaving messages for me at home, or else. And now she was saying the doctor's results had come and she would have to be operated on in three weeks. She was saying her psychiatrist had said she must go back on anti-depressants. She was asking – what was I doing in the queue? How long was it? Was I bored? Who was that young girl at the bakery I had said could keep bread for her? Did I want two litres of cooking oil? How long was this petrol queue? Was it moving? Had there been any delivery yet or were we just waiting? Could she come and keep me company in the queue? Talk to me? Bring me some beers? Tell me about her

retirement package? About her operation? About the anti-
depressants that bloated up her body and made her numb?
About Tariro? Did I think she should send Tariro to boarding
school? Would she then be lonely? Could we talk about Jean's
recent miscarriage? About myself?
I told Rudo not to come. I did not want her to come. She was
wearing me down with her miseries. The last thing I wanted
was somebody wearing me down. I didn't like the way she
went on about Nontokozo and the hot-blooded, high-density
lasses with five borderline O-levels and typing certificates
who were supposedly dying to serve me fried lizards' tails to
soften my brain. Rudo offered me new possibilities, but I didn't
like the way she was crowding me into the little corner of her
snobbishness and prejudice. By the time the tanker arrived, at
seven in the evening, it was too late anyway, and she would be
preparing dinner for Tariro.

When the tanker arrived people banged out of their cars and
scrambled up from the kerbs to gather along the fence of the garage.
A young man rode down past the fence and nonchalantly shouted,
'Diesel only! Diesel only!' A hubbub went up. Was it diesel? Was it
petrol? Was it both? Surely it must be diesel because the last delivery
had been petrol! No, but this green tanker had two compartments, one
for diesel and one for petrol! But was it big enough for that? No, it
wasn't. Yes, it was! But how was that possible? Didn't the two fuels
mix? Oh, but didn't you know the tanker had two divisions inside?
Didn't you know the green tankers had divisions inside? All right, but
how much were they delivering? Four thousand, five thousand litres?
And look at the queue! Two hundred cars at the very least. Would the
delivery be enough for all the cars? Would they give full tanks or half,
or only twenty litres perhaps? Would they serve until the fuel ran out
or would they send the customers away at closing time and tell them to
come again tomorrow? Were garages governed by closing times any
more? And this garage was lucky, wasn't it? Getting deliveries when
others went for weeks without anything. Look, the attendant is dipping
his stick into the two tanks and they should be serving within an hour

or two. Come, guys. Get into your cars and close off all the gaps. Order, patience, people. We'll all get served. Patience please. Gosh, I wish they would issue us tickets so we know who gets served and who doesn't, so those who won't get served don't have to waste their time in the queue. Now look, those stupid kombi drivers are jumping the queue and jamming the entrance and mobbing the policeman! God please no ...

I got served at ten to eight – the day's ration of twenty litres, which would last me three days, but it was better than nothing. I threw money at the attendant, swerved away from the pump, thrust my car in front of a blaring bus, waved back the incredulous driver and inched out past the wall of kombis, into the fresh air. When I got to the school, at eight, the kids were waiting, sitting patiently in the dark, clutching their bags under the trees in the deserted yard. No one said a word as we drove home.

Now I know, Rudo.

I have been queuing up all my life.

I have been sleeping in endless queues, yawning in the tired mornings of my dreams; unwashed and hastily dressed, and naked to abuse; hungry for friendship and tolerance and thirsty for intelligence and respect. I have U-turned into lots of queues, many a wrong queue, only to be told at the crammed garages of my fantasies that I am in the wrong lane, or to be turned away. I have idled in snail-paced queues, burning up my precious juice, only to be sent away with a quarter of my fill. I have waved away kindness and trapped myself among the kombies of my own selfishness.

I'm sorry, Rudo ...

Tavonga

She was about two years old in those days when I first ventured into the ambience of JC's household.

She – Tavonga – fell in love with me at once, and named me, for better or worse, Bhiya, alias Beer. She would fling herself into my lap, snatch my glasses off my nose and toss them onto the display cabinet. And then she would yank up my T-shirt and run a finger over my navel, touching her lips to my nipples, while whispering, *'Kaka, Kaka. Gogo hona kaka waBhiya.'* Finally she would happily help herself to a sip and then another sip from my glass of beer on the coffee table.

'But won't this be a problem later?' I asked, concerned.

'She'll get over it,' JC said half prophetically, tossing her braids. Anyway she'll go straight to sleep and that's a blessing – besides, children who start drinking early always give up.

'Look at you and me. We were raised to see devils with pitchforks in every beer and now look at us, imbibing like fish.'

Tavonga was a bundle of irrepressible energy. You couldn't keep her still. She seemed to be everywhere at once. I said to JC, 'I can't remember, but are all two-and-something-year-olds this active?'

JC said, 'Generally, but this one is hyper.'

As if to confirm her remark, Tavonga grabbed JC's mobile phone and took a swipe at the TV screen, missing it by millimetres.

'Linda!' JC called out. 'Please come and fetch Tavonga.'

Linda, at twenty-two, was slim but ample-bosomed with shapely legs that could have done with a shave. She had a triumphant, half-sly look as she emerged from the spare bathroom, pink soap-suds on her hands. She fished Tavonga out from behind the curtains, capturing her wriggling little body between her legs.

'Change her nappy and her dress and fix her something to eat,' said JC, flipping through the day's newspapers. 'Did she sleep this afternoon or did you let her watch cartoons on TV all day? I'll rock her to sleep when she has eaten.

'What have you made for supper, Linda?'

'There's spaghetti and mince, Mhamha.'

'Did you brown the mince as I showed you last time?'

'Yes, Mhamha. And there's the sour milk Sis Bena brought yesterday from Sekuru Doc's farm.'

'Cream that for desert. Mr Bhiya likes creamed sour milk.'

Tavonga lay on her back pretending to read the newspaper upside-down while mouthing the words. When JC turned to a fresh page, she turned one too. Out in the car park someone clicked their remote control and Tavonga leapt off the sofa, and clambered onto the little bamboo chair I had bought her, to wave through the open window, 'Bena! Bena!' A moment later Bena came in through the door, in a grey executive suit, lugging two paper bags and a laptop. She swept Tavonga off her feet and said, 'Hi Mhamha. Hi, Mr Bhiya. How was your day?'

She dug into one of the bags, pulling out a new denim dress, and then knelt down to try it on Tavonga.

'Perfect,' said JC. 'Where did you find it, Bena?'

'At the flea market in Fourth Street.' Pulling the straps between her fingers, Bena slipped out of her slender black shoes, and planted the laptop on top of the room divider, out of Tavonga's reach. 'There's lots of good stuff there. I didn't have enough cash to buy you or Linda anything. It's amazing, Mhamha, how people will spend a fortune in the so-called departmental stores for stuff that you can buy in the market at half the price.'

Tavonga pranced about the room like a little model. *'Gogo hona ndachena. Hona Bhiya. Hona Bena. Hona Linda ndachena.'*

47

'Did you kneel down and say "Thank you, Aunt Bena?",' JC asked.

Tavonga knelt down and said, 'Thank you, Aunt Bena.'

'Good girl, Tavo.'

'Okay, Tavo,' said Bena. 'Fetch your books and I'll teach you to read. Remember next year you're going to pre-school, baby.'

'Give Mr Bhiya a beer, but don't bring me another, Linda,' JC called while putting a jazz CD on the hi-fi. 'I'm organising a big conference tomorrow for the partners and I need a clear head.'

Linda beamed and I thought she half-winked at me as she opened the fridge.

***

Whenever Linda took Tavonga to JC's office, the child would insist on riding up and down the elevator until the guards tempted her out with the promise of an ice-cream, while Linda watched, half amused.

That small girl possessed an incurable itch to visit people's homes, and she had a way of slipping into cars and hiding behind the back seat until she was fished out, kicking and yelling with shame or despair at being discovered. Once, crouching like a fowl behind the front seat, she was only discovered some twenty kilometres later. The driver, an old friend, had little option but to continue on to his rural home, and accommodate Tavonga for the night. Once there, the child made friends, young and old, sampled melons and *tsvubvu*, herded goats, played *pada* in the moonlight, sipped the ancestral brews, and was brought back home with a glorious parcel of green maize and *nyimo*.

On another occasion, she cried to be allowed to go shopping with the young couple next door. It followed that she returned home with a pail of ice-cream, a new T-shirt, and paraded herself, saying, *'Hona Gogo. Gogo ndachena.'*

If she was spoilt, it was because JC and Bena couldn't help it, she attracted attention. Tavonga was warm, pretty, outgoing, funny, and everybody loved her. She had many husbands. At least the four I knew were Roy, the bubbly accounting partner who lived in the flat below and drove a BMW; taciturn Mark, in Grade 2, who watched cartoons and played at the jumping castle with her; Jacob, the engineer, who often visited his real wife downstairs, although they were half divorced, and with whom JC and I sometimes drank and laughed at a well-known jazz joint while he plied us with his woes and sought our advice; and lastly, myself, the veritable Mr Bhiya of the fascinating tits and navel.

One day Tavonga inadvertently discovered that she had all four husbands in the room together, and like the cheating little wife that she was, she didn't know who to talk to or sit with or what to do.

'See, Tavo,' JC laughed. 'A woman ought to have only one man at a time. And that goes for the man too.'

Tavonga just ran downstairs to play and find new friends.

I said to JC, 'Watch it, Tavo might get abused,' and JC said, 'It's crossed my mind too, but it's not likely to happen.'

I said, 'That little girl is either going to grow into a flirt or a PR genius, JC.'

'Children must be allowed that choice.'

***

When Bena drove them – JC, Linda and Tavonga – to see JC's mother, Gogo Choga, in one of Harare's older suburbs (JC's parents had bought the house soon after independence) Tavonga ventured into the chicken-run and tried to nurse the little chicks. Eventually Gogo Choga tied a towel over Tavonga's shoulder and tumbled the chicks, all fluff and beaks, into the soft hollow between the towel and Tavonga's chest so that the child could rock them, feed them bread and tea, and teach them 'Baba, Black Sheep,' 'One, two, three, four' and *'Ye uuyeu, nyarara mwanawe'*. When the chicks' mother, a rowdy brown hen, cawed loudly in protest, Tavonga stripped a fresh little bough from a mulberry tree and chased her all over the yard. Finally, exhausted, Tavonga freed the chicks and flopped onto a sofa. Gogo Choga gave her *maheu* to drink and she took cautious sips. Revived, she climbed onto the table so that she could be as tall as Gogo Choga. She said to JC, *'Gogo VaTavo, ndipowo bhiya.'*

Gogo Choga said to JC, 'Gogo VaTavo, what on earth have you been doing to this child? Don't tell me you are doing to this child what your late father did to you. Your father went drinking with you when you were very young and now look at you!'

'Come on, mother. My father and I were buddies, and as far as I am concerned there is nothing wrong with me.'

'Maybe if you hadn't taken to drink so early in your life ...?'

'I'd have been married. Is that what you want to say?'

'So, what's wrong with getting married and settling down?'

'Who says marriage is everything there is to life? Who says a man is everything a woman wants? How many women have made it without men? Didn't I raise Bena without her father lifting a finger to help? And didn't my father feed Bena *masese* when she was young? Does she drink today? Ask her.'

'Do you drink, Bena?'

'Gogo Choga, Sis Bena doesn't touch a drop,' Linda vouched for her surrogate sister.

'Gogo Choga,' said Bena. 'Marriage, like drinking, is purely a matter of choice.'

'And you too, Bena, *muzukuru*, think like that. I was looking forward to having great-grandchildren in my lifetime. Now, I give up.'

'Gogo Choga, you should have let my father be,' said JC, with quiet resignation, 'and not quarrelled with him all his life. Tell me, did you and Sekuru Choga ever get on together? Him, the white-haired buddy of the bars and you, *mudzimai weruwadzano?*'

'So you don't think I loved your father? Let me tell you, there are things it takes a lifetime to understand.'

Accompanied by Linda, Bena drove out to buy Gogo Choga's prescription for high blood pressure from the local pharmacy while JC and her mother prepared samp. Bena had earlier driven the old woman to her rural home, two hundred kilometres away, to fetch the maize, and her mortar and pestle. Even before that, she had driven a delivery of fertiliser *kumusha* for Gogo Choga. And then, just last Christmas, Bena had given her grandmother two costumes and a brand new double fridge.

Bena had ...

In the meantime, Tavonga ran about collecting stray maize seeds to feed the now encaged and pacified hen and her brood. She screamed with delight as the sharp little beaks pecked at her palms.

In the evening when the lights suddenly failed, Bena said, 'Whole suburbs in pitch darkness. Imagine! It's so systematic. Whoever is running the energy ministry should be electrocuted.'

'What would you do with whoever is in charge of water purification, Sis Bena?' Linda quizzed.

'Drown him. Or her! Or it!'

'And the minister in charge of collapsing banks?' laughed JC.

'Lock him up in a vault at the reserve bank.'

'And the chef in charge of justice?'

'Hang him from a banana tree.'

'Shhh. You kids. You'll get us locked up.'

'But Gogo Choga, these aren't the sixties or seventies any more. You should learn to speak up. Isn't that why you people fought Ian Douglas Smith and his cronies?'

'And what do you "born frees" know about Ian Douglas Smith, Bena?'

'Enough to get by, Gogo.'

Gogo Choga lit a gas-lamp. Fortunately the food was cooked. Linda helped her serve the brown rice and goat stew.

JC said to Tavonga, 'Pray for us, sweetie,' and they all closed their eyes. Linda whispered in Tavonga's ear and Tavonga bunched her palms together and said, 'Ahhhh,' and they ate.

Tavonga squatted on the carpet and warmed her hands at the lamp. She blew at the wick to make the fire bigger and warmer, and she said to her mother, *'Jiya,* Linda. Gogo *atonhola.'*

Then the lights came back on and the black and white TV burst into life. On the screen a herd of grazing cows appeared in a field. Tavonga knelt down on all fours and grazed off the carpet in imitation.

Gogo Choga fell back on the sofa, laughing.

A mouse – poor creature that must have lodged in some crevice of that ancient house – scuttled across the floor and brushed Tavonga's leg. Yelling with fright, Tavonga leapt out of the door, into the dark night.

'Tavonga!' Bena called, firmly. 'Come back here this minute. Haven't you ever seen a mouse before? Linda, has your child never seen a mouse?'

'*Gogo hona gonjo,*' Tavonga sobbed, appealing from one face to another, tears streaming down her face. She reluctantly ventured back to the lounge. JC embraced her, crooning, 'Come my darling Tavo. Bena, don't do that to my Tavo. Bena, please don't do that now.'

Tavonga nestled in JC's bosom and soon fell asleep.

Gogo Choga started singing a hymn. Linda and Bena picked up the dishes and went to the sink to wash them.

***

Linda and Tavonga had been adopted straight off the streets when Tavonga was only three months old. Linda was then a sour street kid nursing her measly bundle and begging for soup and nappies at a local Pentecostal church when Bena spotted her. The church had launched a request for people willing to adopt the girl and her daughter. The two young women sang and fellowshipped together in the choir group and were drawn together by laughter and youthful belief. They began talking. Bena asked questions, the other slowly lost her reticence. It was said that the man, or boy, who'd made Linda pregnant, had vanished off the streets once the deed was done, though Linda's version was that Tavonga's father had disappeared to the UK. Bena, however, was convinced he must have been a street kid. JC's shrewd conviction was that he was a sugar-daddy who preyed off the alleys.

'Let's adopt them, Mhamha,' Bena urged, with twenty-two-year-old zeal. 'I don't have a brother or sister and Linda is only two years younger than me, poor and needy. We can afford to be generous and I could do with a sister.'

'Would you share your bed, your room, your life with a street kid and her baby? Do you know what that means?' JC probed her gently.

Bena nodded.

JC shrugged off her doubts in a manner at once resigned and liberated and let Bena have her way. Ever since she had been deserted by Bena's father at only twenty-one, she had let her daughter have her way. She had decided that husband or no husband, man or no man, she would look after her child, send her to school, move forward with her career and tell the world to simply piss off. She wasn't a young, effervescent Pentecostal – oh no – in fact she was mildly Anglican, but still she instinctively softened towards Linda because she too had been betrayed and left with a small baby.

And so it came to pass that one night the church people brought Linda and Tavonga to JC's flat, and after lecturing Linda on obedience, gratitude and perseverance, left her sitting on the floor in her torn white T-shirt and broken sneakers, nursing her sniffling, skimpily-dressed baby. Bena searched her wardrobe and offered Linda some clothes, and together they bought milk, cereal, fruit, yoghurt, and medicine to make Tavonga well and in just a few weeks, the baby was big and bouncing and beautiful.

And the Lord saw that it was good, and Bena was blessed with a professional degree, and a prestigious job, and a brand new car at the age of twenty-three.

So, JC became the proud mother of two daughters and grandmother of one, and the inmates of the block marvelled at her wondrous household. And the Lord saw that that too was good and he showered JC with blessings.

***

Linda did the housework, but she was not exactly a maid. She swept, cleaned and cooked, but JC and Bena prided themselves on doing their own laundry and they enjoyed cooking. Later, Linda was sent to night school while JC baby-sat. If the older woman had wanted to keep Linda as a maid in return for looking after her baby, then she did not tell me, and JC was not one to hide things. Or so I thought.

Bena and Linda watched TV together and they argued about the films they'd seen and Bena taught Linda maths, accounts and science. Linda adjusted easily to her new home. She had an easy and adaptable disposition: the street had taught her to survive, and the church had taught her to be polite and modest. If she was confused about her role being both and neither sister and daughter, maid and protegé, she did not show it.

JC basked in the warmth of her generosity, but worried, rightly or wrongly, about the complications of adoption. A young African woman and her baby, both of dubious parentage, rescued from the streets in equally dubious circumstances, with unacknowledged kinfolk, is likely to cause sombre reflections about the unknown even among those of determined good will.

The adoptive parents have to inform their relatives, should anything happen in the future. The adoptee has to be welcomed into the family and brought under the caring wing of the new clan; and accepted by the family spirits as it were. If there are any complications in the adoptee's ancestry, these have to be dealt with sooner or later. In Western culture a man or woman or couple can adopt a beautiful baby without worrying very much about its parentage, or more especially its ancestors, but with the JCs of this world, and there are very few of them, matters are not so straightforward.

JC knew about these complexities, so she told her mother and brothers what she had chosen to do and they said, 'Well, JC, okay. It's your decision.'

Linda's kinfolk were a slow revelation. Her mother was a comrade during the war – that much Linda confessed, and Tariro, one of JC's best friends, now an ex-combatant safely installed in the official army, vouched for that.

'I fought with Linda's mother during the war,' Tariro reminisced. 'I must have done, Linda is the carbon copy of her mother: dark, slim, short with laughing eyes and sly looks. Her mother was always naughty and getting us punished in the barracks but she was a good comrade, a good fighter and she died in a contact just before the cease-fire. God rest her soul.'

Dead comrade. How had Linda's mother died? How many lives had she taken? Could she bring bad luck? Had she been cleansed after the war or had the generality of war absolved her people from that? Did people from the war need to be cleansed? Would her dead mother now say, 'Thank you JC for looking after my child,' or would she sulk incomprehensibly? Could Linda bring bad luck?

Was Linda a war child? Had she been born in the struggle, raised in the refugee camps and then let out onto the streets?

JC fretted. She was, as we've said, a sensible woman and an educated professional but she knew, like most sensible Africans, that some things simply could not be wished away.

And so one Sunday morning JC decided that the time had come – it had to – and insisted that Linda search out her grandmother, and her siblings, to re-establish, or perhaps more realistically, establish links. JC wanted Linda to explain where she was living, and she hoped her relatives would give their blessing. One could never be sure. She gave the young woman money and some groceries and Bena drove them to the market place and made sure they got on the bus.

For two long weeks the flat was quiet. There was no Tavonga to break things, no one to scream at, no one to cuddle, no one to bring presents to. JC and Bena became irritable. They realised wryly how much and how richly Linda and Tavonga had become a part of their lives. Without their presence they felt more exposed to each other's needs, and there was no cushion to soften their mutual dependency. They knew how much the girl and her daughter had fulfilled them individually, and as a family unit.

Linda returned two weeks later from the rural areas looking thoroughly emaciated, with a sick and feverish Tavonga. She brought scant news of a surviving twin sister and unconfirmed reports of an older brother working in white people's yards in the city. JC had hoped for more. She had wanted, needed, peace of mind and she was angry that she could not prise any more out of Linda. In her anxiety she felt that somehow Linda was taking advantage of her. She knew she was not being rational, she was the stronger party and could throw Linda out if she chose to do so, but still she imagined that the girl was holding something back. 'If she doesn't tell the truth she will have to go, Mhamha,' Bena said, picking up on her mother's irritation and feeling ill at ease because she was the one who had brought Linda and Tavonga into their home. In many ways she considered herself a modern woman, but she too was prey to the fear that Linda's relatives might suddenly arrive and make unexpected demands.

'And what will happen to little Tavonga, then?' said JC. 'Look what has happened to them both, in just two weeks. How long will it take us to nurse the child back to health? Do you want her to go to the rurals and die of malaria or diarrhoea after all these months of care? What will you have achieved, then?'

'Mhamha, you love that baby too much.'

'No, Bena, you love her too much!'

'You can't give her up because you have done so much for her. And Mhamha, you know what? Linda came back with only one dress. She must have sold off the others she took with her.'

'Gave them to her twin sister, most likely,' JC said with her accustomed insight.

'And to think those were dresses that I gave her. If she needed to give them to her twin sister why didn't she just ask?'

If they'd hoped for a satisfactory resolution to the niggling anxiety of ancestry and dubious relatives, they felt short-changed.

Linda did not offer any convincing explanation. Perhaps she was protective of herself and her people. Perhaps what had transpired in the rurals was too big for her to broach herself, let alone attempt to explain to her somewhat naïve benefactors. After all, people at the receiving end of charity need not always excuse themselves. Destitutes must sometimes be allowed to have minds of their own. Linda had tasted the desolation of the streets and confronted the relentless anger of the world; she was, like her mother, streetwise. Perhaps her people had said, 'How dare this woman and her daughter try to own you and your baby. Are they trying to buy you out of our hands? Is money and good living thicker than blood? Don't they realise we can just marry you off one of these fine days?' Why had she got so thin, had they not fed her?

Bena wanted an explanation. She felt it was owed to her. She was aware, against her better instincts, that she longed for submissive gratitude, a reassurance that they had done the right thing.

Bena kept Linda at arm's length for a week. And in justifying her sense of betrayal, if that is what it was, she remembered other simmering complaints, like special toiletries missing from both bedrooms. Like a diminishing stock of empty beer bottles in the pantry. Like an ever-escalating phone bill even from a locked telephone. Like Linda being absent from the flat for long stretches of the day. Like reports of Linda entertaining young male visitors in the flat during the day. Like Linda bunking night school lessons and not handing over all required fees …

Like …

Bena moved out to stay with a friend for a couple of days.

To be honest, JC confessed, Bena sometimes acted big-headedly, treating Linda like a domestic and flaunting her car and everything.

Despite the tense atmosphere, Linda shrewdly realised that she would never be sent away, and that Bena was torn between the contradictions of power and generosity, so she stood her ground. She didn't have to tell if she didn't want to.

JC had a serious talk with Linda, then with the church-goers who had brought her and they in turn had a serious talk with the young woman. Linda, apologising, promised not to take anything else without asking first. Then Bena suddenly returned home with parcels and presents and the antagonism between them thawed; the two young women would drive again, like sisters, to church services and prayer meetings or to the ice-cream den and the park, and there was laughter again in the flat.

**

And where was I in all this? Who was I and what was I? Why and how was I?

Well, I wasn't anybody at that time.

Was I anybody, then?

Well, I hadn't seen my born-again spouse for months, and we had fought again about loyalty, money, responsibilities, beliefs, sex and egos, and this time she had said she was going for good and now she was holed up in that damned flat fellowshipping ten times a week with Godknowswho and I was marooned at the house with the kids, the school fees, the grocery bills and my smashed-up fantasies, and I was dithering with startling possibilities and my favourite, favourite daughter Number 2 sobbed up a storm when I tried to get her to share her bedroom with the maid and as usual I gave in. So my daughter was ordering the maid about and I didn't know what to do when I heard that my favourite, favourite daughter number 1, who was studying down south, had saved enough from the fees I had sent her to fly herself to London for a holiday and she hadn't even brought home a T-shirt for anyone, while all my jeans were bursting at the seams and there was no one to sew them up and as always it was my teenage son who was staying at home watching DSTV and holding the fort, always my son scrambling eggs for me on Sunday evenings and I wondered why there were no jokes or laughter or gossip within my walls and nothing but ambition and selfishness and snobbery in this house of no music, no drinks, no visitors and I said, was it my fault for being so stern or had I been too busy fending for my kids to see the rot creeping in or had the laughter been wrung out of me and I thought that all I had then was my son or should I have myself cloned? And I thought to myself, why, but I have friends all over the world and some people think I'm a really nice person.

And my sisters and my friends were saying you are somebody, stop feeling sorry for yourself and stop killing yourself with drink and forget her if she doesn't deserve you and get up and spruce yourself up and be yourself again, for God's sake dump her if she makes you miserable, if you don't love yourself nobody is going to love you, get up and do what we know you can do best.

And then you, JC, came along the street and bumped into me outside the pharmacy and we recognised each other and talked about old times and I said I last saw you ten, maybe fifteen years ago, but I first knew you twenty years ago when you were a very slim actress going for book-keeping lessons with my high school sweetheart Letwina and oh, how I liked you then and I bought you drinks and took your number but forgot to phone and the next time I saw you was at Philemon's party with that comical dark man who made you laugh so much and you said he was only a friend; and I waved once or twice at you when you were still a junior working with my wife and I said outside the pharmacy, 'My, my, you've put on weight and have become a real madam, costumes and shoes and umbrella and all,' and you laughed back and said, 'What about that maize meal on your head and that pot belly?' and you asked, 'Is it money or stress?' and I said, 'Both,' and you laughed and gave me your card and I said, 'Can I take you out for a drink?' and you said, 'Well, all right.'

Then next I was at the Eyre Gardens talking to you and telling you about myself and you were nodding softly, half believing me, smiling and sipping your drink and I took you home early because you were going to work and I came again at the weekend and this time you allowed me into your flat and I said, 'Wow! What a large beautiful place you have,' and I said, 'Hi' to Bena, while Linda and Tavonga watched me tentatively from behind the curtain, sizing me up and I said, 'Are these your children?' and you said, 'Yes,' and I asked Bena, 'Is Linda your sister?' and she said, 'Yes,' and I said, 'Bena looks more like you,' and you said, 'Must all children look like their mother?' and I said, 'Tavonga is too young to be your daughter,' and you said 'She's my grandchild,' and I said, 'So you are a grandma,' and you said, 'Yes, Sir,' and I said to Bena, 'Can I love your mother?' and she said, 'Yes, if you wish,' and I said, 'Does any man visit this place?' and Bena innocently said, 'Nobody I know of right now.'

And you later said, 'I didn't know you were such a nice person.'

So I started visiting your flat regularly. Like Linda and Tavonga I surfaced, stained from the streets, at your door and you instantly adopted me. I shared your sumptuous food, your brainy music, your TV, your newspapers, your bed. You ransacked your wardrobe for T-shirts to clothe me. You were the Stopayne for my headache and the Imodium for my belly. You washed my stuff, packed my clothes and had Linda ready with hot breakfasts in the morning when you were late for work and left me behind, dozing off my hangovers in your bed.

I said, 'You're stealing me from her, aren't you?' You said, 'Not when she has deserted you like this.'

I said, 'What if she takes you to court?' You said, 'For what?'

I said, 'What if she sends thugs to beat you up, or shoot you, or cut you up, or rub pepper between your legs?' And you said, 'Don't I have hands too?'

I said, 'Do you realise you're stealing me from my children?' And you said, 'How do you know? Maybe they're actually happy when you're away, what with your constant tirades against them and your ranting and frustrations about their mother.'

Yes, you said all the right things and had everything in place for me. You were the perfect 'small house' and I had never really had a small house before.

You were a seeping well of knowledge. You had answers for everything. You seemed to know everything. You were generous

59

beyond compare. You fed newspaper boys and caretakers and security guards tea, orange juice and sandwiches, hosted your brother's friends and, yes, you even baked a birthday cake for Tavonga's third husband, my arch rival Mark.

Then, as with Linda and Tavonga, you started wanting to know about me. You wondered what you considered an eligible man like me was doing in the streets, why I was unattached. You knew my wife, yes, you had even worked with her once, and in your generosity you even described her as a beautiful woman. You wondered what had come between us but never pushed your questions.

Like Linda, I wriggled free of your inquiry.

We braaied our weekends away and feasted on Simply Red, The Lighthouse Family, Earl Klugh, Sankomota, Yondo Sister and Sade. Sometimes I invited out your friends to broaden our circle and they joined us – Tariro the ever-ready battery, Sheila the sponge, Bea your serene receptionist. We even took your brother Kay twice for a drink and he relished our company. There was no class or age limit to your friends. You looked for the good in people and turned a blind eye to the bad. We bantered hilariously with small-time vegetable farmers and bottle-store belles. We interviewed dissipated chiefs, fat-headed herbalists and pimple-faced evangelists in stunning robes and bought *mitsvairo* and *migoti* and *mboora* from gratified roadside wives. We quizzed brash teenage prostitutes and sly-eyed pickpockets and garrulous layabouts; you left genuine phone numbers for desperate, aspiring messengers and clerks who mistook your eagerness for frivolity and never showed up for the interviews you arranged for them.

At the Jazz Club we befriended the likes of Dudu Manhenga and Prudence Katomeni, Summer Breeze and Bob Nyabinde, and who is that man in the papers who always sneaked up behind your seat and held your head in his hands and pecked you on the ear? And that bumptious proprietress with a mile-long trail of perfume behind her who hugged every customer but never, never me and half believed you were six months' pregnant until she squeezed your belly? And good old Walter, the book-keeper, earnest with his yarns, forever boasting at three on Saturday mornings that he adored his wife who was bent on doing a second Ph.D., Walter insisting on buying round after round and relieving his purse on us even when you tried to stop him.

Who were they all? What is it they liked about you, about us? What were their problems? Why did they let us assail them so easily with our mere presence?

We did not realise what we were doing but I now think that we were seeking not just to understand different people, but to cut our frail teeth on the seasoned biltong of human nature. You taught me in your household and in our excursions, no, reminded me, me the recluse, me the self-pitying wimp, me the unrepentant hypocrite, about the largeness of life and the generosity of openness; about the relatedness of disparateness, about the beautiful fusion of friendship and common sense.

Did you teach me about the salient tragedy of charity? About the intricacies of small houses?

You confirmed to me the infallible likeness of generations – Linda's mother and Linda and Tavonga; you and Bena; my wife and my daughters; me and my son.

Like the administrator you are, you had a knack for faces, names, places, details and you complemented my sometimes crude impressionism. On Sundays you sent me back, just as you sent Linda, to search out members of my fractured family. You requested names, ages, idiosyncrasies, personalities and you stored up every detail I told you. You spoke of my children like your own. Like Linda, I told you a lot but I didn't tell all. I flitted on peripheries. I avoided the dirty little pasts and the persistent presences that would banish me from your grace. As you listened to Tavonga prattling, so you listened to my squeamish, overgrown pleas about myself; you soothed my persistent aches for respect and recognition with your elaborate lotions and creams. You let me rant on about my spouse without seeming to take sides. You respected me, were proud of me, read my every sentence, e-mailed me, sent me cuttings when I was away. You were open, generous, forgiving and trusting – you seemed to have nothing to hide. If this was your way of winning me over you were a genius, like your grandchild Tavonga. Dangerously, recklessly, I revealed more and more about myself.

***

Yet at times it seemed you were too good to be true. Who had you been going out with in the twenty years before you met me? It seemed at times you were finicky about my life. Were you not now disregarding the fine boundaries between 'small' and 'real' houses, which you yourself had taught me? What was the real depth of your generosity? What were your motives?

Whenever my phone rang, you did not say anything, but I could feel your eyes asking for more. And always when you went to work in the morning and left me behind in your bed, you would phone to find out if I was up and what Linda was doing. You knew my weakness for women, but I hope to God that you didn't think there was anything going on between Linda and me but the lessons I gave her. God. Please, no!

Tavonga was the buffer. Between Bena and Linda. Between you and Linda. Between you and Bena. Between you and me.

Now she was three. She could say 'whoops' instead of 'wupisi' or salad in place of 'koradi'. She would sense when my absences grew too long and would say, 'Gogo, where is Bhiya?' And when I turned up, she would say, 'Where were you, Bhiya? Gogo was looking for you.' And sometimes when I was not there, she would wake up in the middle of the night, leaving Bena and Linda asleep, slip into your bedroom and climb up into your huge arms and rub her little navel against yours as if realising the essence of touch.

***

'I talked to Linda on the phone,' I tell you, and you stare at me stonily.

Linda has been at it again, reportedly inviting male guests to the flat, cooking for them, serving them drinks and playing them CDs while Tavonga was playing, half-dressed and unwashed, in the flats downstairs.

You glance at me and look away and say nothing. Of late we have become irritable with each other. We both realise that the subject of Linda is only tangential, that we should be grappling with the more complex geometry of our relationship.

'I only did it for your sake,' I say. 'I told her that she was taking advantage of you. I thought maybe she would listen to me. You know I get on well with her.'

You take out your cellphone and fidget with it.

'Look,' I said. 'She's only twenty-two.'

You empty your quart of Pilsener through the open window of the car and look at your watch in the half light. At the fires, figures are milling around the braai and a few couples are dancing on the stage. An open twin cab half a dozen cars to the left is competing with the disco.

'Look,' I begin again. 'She's only twenty-two and she has serious image problems. On the one hand she respects you – she's not really a disrespectful child, not even what you'd call naughty. On the other she feels she's part of your family and she can do what she wants. She's probably going around telling people you are her real mother, and why not? But I wonder how Tavonga will feel when she grows up and learns the truth.'

I take a sip from my almost full quart.

'Look, she was still a teenager when she fell pregnant. Her youth was cut short. She is still a child, you know, aching for boyfriends and fun and all that. I told her she has to respect you, and do what you tell her, and get on with school and get a certificate and a job and look after herself and her child. I told her Bena and you can't take care of her forever.'

You look at the floor of the car and say nothing.

'Would you like pork?' I ask, and you shake your head slightly. Pork chops are your favourite dish.

'Another Pilsener?' Again you shake your head.

'Do you want to go home now?'

You look at your watch.

I start the car and ease out of the crowded grounds, onto the dust track. A full, fat, lonely, yellow moon is rising. I do not turn on the music. A lost calf bleats in the field. We drive for half an hour without talking. At a bridge where a truck plunged over and was submerged, killing its occupants and lying miraculously undiscovered for eleven months, I nearly lose control of the car and brake sharply. Your palms snap open on the dashboard.

'I'm sorry,' I mutter. You know I'm a good driver.

We get to your block and I lock up the car and sombrely follow you up the stairs to your flat.

At the door Tavonga welcomes us. 'Good evening Gogo. Good evening Bhiya. How are you, Gogo? How are you, Bhiya?' Bena has been doing a terrific job teaching her English and songs and Bible verses. She no longer drinks beer. She no longer rushes around smashing things. She now happily helps Linda clear the table and clean up. Bena is convinced she should go to crèche.

Tavonga throws her arms around your knees and you sweep her up into your arms.

'Hi, Tavo. How are you my darling Tavo?'

Linda comes out of the bedroom clad in a purple track suit and penitently clutching a biology text book. I remember I offered to help her with some of her subjects but she procrastinated. Now her results will be out in two weeks and God knows how she fared. Her eyes meet mine and she looks aside. I have again offered to teach her English and Bena has been talking of finding her a job as an office orderly.

'*Maswera sei mhamha? Maswera sei mukwasha?*'

I sit on my favourite sofa and take a sip from my now warm beer.

'Shall I warm up the food for you, Mhamha? There's oxtail and mashed potatoes.'

You hug and kiss Tavonga and she nestles in your arms. Sensing the unusual silence, Linda withdraws to the bedroom.

'Did Tavonga eat, Linda?'

'She had beans and potatoes,' Linda replies. 'You know she doesn't like meat.'

'She's sleeping now. I'll bring her later.'

'Bena was shocked and ashamed at you.' You turn on me without warning. 'Last Saturday when you phoned to say you were sick, and she saw you parked at a bottle store with a woman younger than Linda. Here was little Bena, thinking you are her mother's best friend and buying you T-shirts and birthday presents and you trample her heart like that. Even her own boyfriend wouldn't do that to her and he is an executive at twenty-six. He respects me. Have you ever seen him in here?'

I say nothing. I want to warn you that Bena is too good to find a man to match her and that she will be disappointed but I'm too deep in trouble to issue any more warnings.

'Please stop lecturing me about Linda,' you continue. 'What a flimsy cover-up. You know nothing about that child. You know nothing about your own children. Maybe you don't even know yourself. I don't mean to hurt you. And I didn't mean to tell you this. That night we came from the jazz show at four and you slept like a log your cellphone rang and rang and rang and I couldn't make you wake up and I was worried it might be your children or something wrong at home and I foolishly answered it and a woman rudely asked who I was and what I was doing with you. The confidence in that voice!'

I want the floor to cave into a big hole and cover me up.

'Look, when I met you I took you in because I thought you were lonely and needed to be looked after and I made it clear that I can only have one man at a time. If it was your wife you were going back to I would understand. I gave you all the freedom you wanted and now you are playing teenage games with me. Don't think because I'm in my forties, I'm done for. I have men pestering me every day, some who would make you look like a little boy.'

You lay the now sleeping Tavonga on the sofa and cover her with a blanket. Her little limbs sprawl mindlessly over the edge of the seat. Then you pick up your cellphone. Your face has an expression I have never seen. I think you want to cry; I'm sure you want to cry; I've never seen you cry – even when your grandma died – but I don't know if that glint in your eyes spells defiance.

I do want to say I'm sorry, JC, but my mouth is suddenly dry.

***

In the morning Bena, Linda and Tavonga are getting ready to go to church and you and I are debating whether or not to go to the Domboshawa caves. You are wearing the denim dress I bought you in Italy and I realise that my subtle wish is for you to lose weight. Tavonga is kicking about in her breakfast chair which is now almost too small for her and saying, 'Linda, Linda, where's my daddy? I want a daddy. Bhiya, when are you going to marry Gogo so that I can wear a white dress and carry flowers? Bena, Bena, is your boyfriend taking us for ice-cream today?'

You chew your lower lip in that thoughtful way of yours, contemplating alternatives. Bena goes to her bedroom to search for her car keys. Linda beams at me and then says to Tavonga, 'Eat your eggs quietly, Tavo. And don't speak with food in your mouth.'

The Car

It was a sparkling white VW Golf 1300 with sea grey wind deflectors, silver sports wheel covers, black mudflaps and, of course, a blue and white South African number plate. Thirty-two-year-old Lydia, heavy with her third pregnancy, cheeks rouged and forehead glowing with glistening good health, hair done up in a resplendent dome, swerved the car up the short, narrow, two-track driveway and screeched to a stop just in front of the kitchen.

Tooting loud and long, Lydia eased herself out of her seat. Her mother, Mai Lydia, flung her matronly Saturday morning print cloth round her still capable waist and rushed through the kitchen into the yard. She sketched a dainty little Jerusarema dance, as if mocking the ground and kissing the air, leaping nimbly and ululating. Snatching up the keys that were held out to her, she embraced her daughter.

'Baba Lydia, Baba Lydia,' she yelled to her husband. 'Come out and see.'

Baba Lydia, who was assiduously marking pupils' books in the lounge, stepped out to take a look, scratching a modest pot-belly and sucking his fine teeth. He obviously had a premonition of this event and couldn't therefore look too surprised.

'Baba, Mhamha,' Lydia said triumphantly, 'This is what your son-in-law Roderick has bought you for Christmas.'

'All the way from South, Lydia?'

'Yes, Mother.'

'Oh Roderick, Roderick!'

'Well you two, what are you waiting for? Why don't you jump in for the inaugural ride?'

Mai Lydia leapt into the front passenger seat beside her daughter and her husband slid in behind them. Lydia started the car. The engine coughed, and then kicked into life.

'Roderick bought it from a white lady he works with in Jo'burg,' Lydia explained, brushing a stray lock of human hair from her eyes as she reversed into the street. 'It was an excellent bargain. The car has had one owner all its life. You won't get anything like this in Zimbabwe.'

'Such nice seats,' beamed Mai Lydia, waving at the neighbours who came out to ogle. 'They almost look like *real* leather.'

'So what year is it?' Baba Lydia asked.

'Late eighties, I think. Roderick would know.'

'And the mileage?'

'Seventy thousand ks.'

'Some garages tamper with mileages,' interjected her father darkly.

'The interior and the dashboard are very neat,' Mai Lydia sighed, her eyes alight with joy. 'You can tell it's been well looked after. One-owner cars are usually best.'

'I drove it all the way from Jo'burg by myself and it gave me absolutely no trouble,' Lydia crowed.

'Well, Baba Lydia, you'll have to get a provisional driver's licence fast!'

'What about you, Mother?'

'Oh, didn't I tell you, Lydia? I passed my driver's test two months ago.'

'Great, Mother! So you can teach Father.'

'Watch those children, Lydia,' Baba Lydia's voice was sharp as two infants tore from the grip of an unwary adult and streaked purposelessly across the road. Lydia braked sharply, hooting as she pulled to a halt.

'You'd think people in suburbs might take better care of their children on the roads,' Mai Lydia complained.

To be honest, the car was not exactly Roderick's Christmas present to his wife's parents, but a belated first installment of his lobola. He had paid 'damages' in cash for illicitly making Lydia pregnant: *makativhuna musana masikati machena*, 'stepping on our bare backs in the naked sunlight,' his in-laws had insisted, with suitably wounded decorum. He then delivered the requisite smart clothes and the customary boot full of groceries to demonstrate his good intentions. But, after that, Roderick had fallen quiet. He had reneged on his promises (like so many suitors before him) to promptly deliver the mother's heifer, alive and clip-clopping to their very doorstep. (Hadn't they agreed the father's six beasts could each follow later, as the children were born, a beast or two per child?)

And now, two and a half babies later (nearly three!), here was a car; an unexpected present from a son-in-law who had taken the gap (like so many hungry Zimbabweans) and gone to work down South; here was an automobile squatting fatly in their yard, a magical animal of metal, glass and rubber, an un-quantifiable gift. How much was it worth? The mother's heifer, a heifer and a father's beast, a heifer and two and a half beasts, perhaps?

The matter was contentious.

Baba Lydia raised his head and sniffed at the damp air like a trapped bullock, glared at the sly metallic monster and returned to his pupils' books. He had never been one to acquire gadgets and a car was no exception. After all, he didn't have a driving licence and after fifty-five years of a relatively quiet life he did not see any reason to want one.

In the yard, Mai Lydia felt the sudden pressing need to claim the car as her own; a gift passed on from a doting son-in-law through her daughter. A neighbour popped by and the two women washed the car thoroughly, pouring buckets of warm soapy liquid over it, wiping and polishing every surface and dusting every nook. Lydia, meanwhile, sank heavily into a garden chair, sipping a Mazoe orange and chatting with them, offering her mother tips.

'You might need to have the clutch cable looked at.

'...The battery water will need topping up.'

After Lydia had left, Mai Lydia locked up the car. There was a power cut again, a regular nightly event. The blackout swallowed up the houses and the streets, piling up densely against the damp dark windows, threatening another night of a thousand thieves. Mai Lydia lit the candles, pumped up the feeble paraffin stove, peeked into the frothing pot of beans and said, 'We could build a new garage!'

'There go our six-month back pay and bonuses, if we ever get them,' grumbled Baba Lydia.

'The Salary Service Bureau said that our cheques will be deposited next week. I'll tell you what, Baba Lydia, we could put up a pre-cast wall round the house...'

'Really?'

'Or hire a guard...'

'Safeguard?'

'No. A cheap night guard from the townships... '

'A spindly school leaver with two O-levels, a catapult, pockets full of stones, and the courage of a puppy?'

'He could sleep in the car at night and raise a shout if there's trouble.'

'He'd need to be guarded *himself*!'

'Or we could get an alarm and an immobiliser fixed onto the car.'

'I thought all South African cars came with those extras, given their rate of car thefts. And would you be able to pay for them with your miserable earnings from extra weekend lessons?'

'I'm only trying to *think*, Baba Lydia, and you aren't being very helpful. You've been griping all day; even Lydia and Mai Nyasha noticed. The least you could do is show gratitude to your daughter's husband.'

'A proper son-in-law pays proper lobola and doesn't try to evade his dues with *flimsy* second-hand presents.'

'This car is a *flimsy* present then, is it? How come in all your thirty solid years of teaching you haven't been able buy yourself even a flimsy bicycle?'

'I never asked for a second-hand car.'

'Because you don't have a licence, that's why. You've never done anything to improve your lot, Baba Lydia. ... Well, you're the man of the house. Why don't you take a blanket and go and sleep in the car until the lights come back on?'

'Me? Never. I have a bedroom, and a proper house at that. Besides, I have my pupils' tests to mark. I don't teach infants, you know.'

'There you go again. You think teaching Grade 1s is any easier than teaching Grade 7s! If you'd gone on to add a degree to your teaching certificate and done more child psychology, you'd know better than that!'

'And what has your little degree done for you then? Why aren't you a teacher-in-charge or deputy headmistress?'

'At least I have the degree and when the need for it arises I'll use it.'

'Are we arguing about that again, Mai Lydia?'

'No, we're talking about the car!'

'Second-hand cars, watered down B.Ed. degrees, what's the difference?'

'Ts,ts,ts. Well, Mr Grade 7 teacher, sir, here's your supper.'

'Sadza and beans again.'

'Maybe if you had a degree and found a better job, we'd eat more decent meals in this house.'

'Oh, shut up.'

'If you won't go out there to guard the car I'll do so myself. You can wash up after eating and show a little sense. And don't wait up for me.'

Mai Lydia slammed a plastic plate of steaming food on the table in front of him, fetched a blanket from the bedroom, picked up her supper and went out into the yard. Moments later he heard a car door close softly. But, when he peeped out, he only saw the blurry white form of the vehicle. Morosely, he ate his supper, marked the few remaining books, and wormed his way into the cluttered bedroom. He undressed, climbed into bed, blew out the candle and tried to sleep.

Damn it, he thought, butting his head into the pillow and hugging himself with his arms. He'd had to wait two whole weeks for her and now this!

He must have slept for two or so hours when he woke with a start. There was tapping on the window and his wife was whispering urgently.

71

'Baba Lydia, Baba Lydia!'

'What?'

'Come out and check. There are people in the street, near our gate.'

'So what?' he snorted half sleepily, opening the window. 'It's supposed to be a public street, isn't it?'

'There are two or three men near our gate. Listen.'

Baba Lydia thrust his head out of the window. He saw and heard nothing in the dark.

'If you come out and they hear your voice maybe they'll go away.'

'Why don't you drive the car round and park it next to the bedroom window?'

'Okay. Can you come and direct me?'

Climbing back into the car, she fumbled with the ignition and the lights. He waved his arms in the suddenly blinding beams. Revving noisily, she moved the VW next to the bedroom window.

'Mind the covo!' he hissed, banging a hand on the bonnet. Too late. The wheels of the car grazed down a row of the flourishing vegetables. In a panic, she stepped out and peered through the darkness. Then she carefully locked the car, closed the back door, and finally came to bed. When he tried to hold her she turned aside and moved away from his touch. Two or three times during the night, he woke up and saw her peeking out through the window at the car. He turned aside, with his hands nested between his warm thighs.

***

In the morning she was up early, giving the car one final polish as if for an exhibition. He ate his breakfast silently, then gathered up his books and pens and walked out.

'Baba Lydia, wait,' she implored. It was threatening to rain.

'It's not far to the school,' he said. 'And I need the exercise.'

She put on her best orange suit, hat and shoes, which Roderick had bought her, applied a sweet perfume and stepped out to the car. Dressed up, she definitely looked younger than her fifty years, spruce like a middle-aged mother at her daughter's wedding. As she was reversing, she grazed down another row of covo and narrowly missed a gate-post. Righting her hat, she tried to concentrate. She caught up

72

with her husband at the school gate, slowed down, opened the window and pleaded, 'Won't you at least get in, Baba Lydia? What will the other teachers say?'

'Let them say what they want,' he retorted, marching on.

At the school, the pupils and teachers had already gathered for the open-air assembly. There was a buzz in the air and all faces turned towards her when she arrived. Excited little fingers pointed as she propelled the immaculate Golf past three old cars into the only sheltered bay in the car park. A slow applause gathered as she alighted and clink-clonked in her high heels to the assembly point.

***

Halfway through her second lesson, the school messenger summoned her to the headmaster's office. Here, the old man adjusted the cuffs of his frayed grey shirt, placed his brown, bone-rimmed, thick-lensed glasses on his bare table and gulped for air like an exhausted toad.

'Morning, Mai Lydia,' he began.

'Morning, sir.'

'How was your weekend?'

'Fine, sir, and yours?'

'Fine, fine. And how are things at home, Mai Lydia?'

'Fine, sir. Very fine.'

'I see you drove a new VW Golf into the car park this morning. Is it yours?'

'Yes, it's mine sir. I mean *ours,* sir. My husband's and mine, sir.'

'Oh, congratulations. I see you've been working hard giving extra lessons, then. Or perhaps you have been going down South to buy and sell? Or you found a little gold, or picked up a diamond at Chiadzwa? Who knows? Deals, you know? Who's not doing them these days? Once upon a time our profession was revered, but now a vegetable vendor is better off than a school head. '

'It was a present from my son-in-law, sir.'

'Oh! A present! How nice. I haven't driven a car in five years, since the gearbox of my old Datsun 120Y packed up. And do you have a driver's licence?'

'Yes, sir.'

'And Baba Lydia?'

'Not yet, sir.'

'You mean he can't drive and you can?'

'Yes, sir.'

'Will you teach him to drive, then?'

'I suppose so, sir.'

'Well, well, Mai Lydia. The reason I called you is to remind you that the sheltered parking bay is reserved for the school head, or for visiting dignitaries.'

'I only parked there because it was going to rain, sir.'

'I know, I know. But any time a chef can pop in. An education officer or the Provincial Director, or even the Minister herself, you see. The VIP bay should always be kept free.'

'Very well, sir. I'll take the car out of the bay,' she said, and like a lamb went out to do so.

At breaktime the other teachers flocked to the car park and crowded around the car in admiration. She felt a little flustered, in her suit, hat and high heels, showing them the Golf. Baba Lydia was nowhere to be seen, marking books in the little storeroom behind his 'base'.

After the morning shift, he stayed behind to coach the senior athletics team then strolled to the shops to shake himself free of his discomfiture. When he arrived home after sunset, his wife had already parked the car outside the bedroom window.

'Look at this,' he shook his head mournfully at their little garden. 'The covo is a mess. Now you'll have to buy cabbages at the market.'

He ate moodily and sank heavily onto the bed in the candlelight. When she came to bed she sniffed at him and winced, 'So, have you started drinking again, Baba Lydia? I thought you'd quit that habit years ago.' When she joined him, he did not try to touch her, but turned away.

***

Three or four days later, he woke up to her screams at dawn. 'Baba Lydia! Baba Lydia! The car! The car!'

Now what? Groggily, he stepped out to the yard, into the early morning sunlight and gaped at the VW. The wind deflectors had been unscrewed, and the wheel covers, mudflaps and wipers were missing! He cautiously tried all the doors and the boot; they were firmly locked. Looking inside, the vehicle appeared okay, but the exterior had been visibly despoiled.

'Don't touch the car,' she warned him too late.

She called the nearby police station on her mobile phone. Several hours later, an officer arrived on foot, hatless and uncombed, took notes and asked a few matter-of-fact questions. When had they bought the car? Had they heard any noise during the night? Who had noticed the theft first? Did they suspect anybody? Was the car insured? Shouldn't they perhaps find a neighbour with an empty lock-up garage? Or buy a guard dog? He did not take fingerprints, and vaguely cautioned the couple to report to the station if they discovered any leads.

When the white Golf pulled into the car park late that morning, Mai Lydia driving and her husband plunked miserably beside her, staring obliviously out of the window, the headmaster was waiting outside the staffroom, chewing an arm of his old spectacles, eyeing his wrist watch.

***

Baba Trevor, the deputy headmaster, who lived up their street, offered them his unused garage. His wife had died three years ago in just another horrible kombi accident and people said he had sold his old Datsun Pulsar to offset the expenses of her funeral. His garage had lock-up doors; he had two dogs, and there was an invincible looking pre-cast wall right round his yard. He was a sprightly, well-dressed, ambitious young chap, of maybe forty, and definitely destined for greatness. Recently degreed, he had been a Grade 7 teacher with Baba Lydia before he was promoted to deputy, a position for which the two men had both applied. Twice or thrice he had recommended Mai Lydia for the post of teacher-in-charge of the infants. It was she who had approached him about the matter of the car, of course, and at first he saw nothing wrong with the proposal.

'Would this arrangement be okay with Baba Lydia?'

'There shouldn't be any problem.'

'I'll just confirm the agreement with him then.'

So, like the good colleague he was, Baba Trevor consulted Baba Lydia, who said, cryptically, 'Yes, if you and my wife think so.' So deputy head asked Mai Lydia again, 'Are you sure this is all right with your husband?' and Mai Lydia, shrugging, replied, 'Well, Baba Trevor, you know Baba Lydia…'

Nonetheless, Mai Lydia parked the car every evening in Baba Trevor's garage, retrieving it in the morning when, inevitably, they had to give the deputy a ride to school. The arrangement seemed prudent. Now, most mornings, Baba Lydia rode in the car beside his wife, albeit silently, the deputy behind them, and the woman felt almost gratified. In the afternoons, Baba Lydia preferred to stroll home, stopping off at the shops on his way back. One night, when he was particularly late, Mai Lydia detected the crude sweet musk of cheap perfume mixed with the smell of cigarette smoke and for once she felt numb with anxiety.

No, Petros, this time I WON'T budge. I WON'T be intimidated by your slimy tricks. I am not the one who said, 'Don't go to university and get a degree, don't get a driving licence, don't improve your lot.' Why do you let other men do better than you? These days you have to improvise shrewdly. Zimbabwe is almost impossible now; if you sit on your hands, unofa uchidya nhoko dzezvironda, *you will surely die on the miserly stinking pellets of your wounds, as they say. This car I will drive for sure.* Kutyei? *What should I fear? Didn't I give birth to a daughter? And whoever said the father gets seven or eight beasts for lobola while the mother gets only one heifer needs to have his head examined. Did you carry a child in your womb for nine months? Did you wear a maternity dress? Did you scream, bleed and weep in the maternity ward? Or did you say, 'Chance given!' and sneak off to your girlfriends? Did you suckle Lydia for two years; hoist her to your back? Did you wash nappies? When she suffered from* nhova *did you seek out the old women herbalists in Seke Village? For sure you've oppressed me enough,* shamwari. *If it wasn't for you, I would have listened to my friends and taken promotion in the rural areas, returning to Harare as a deputy head like everyone else. Or gone to Botswana or South Africa to take up a better job. Now, if a vacancy arises, I will leave you to cook for yourself and wash your own clothes. Haven't you got hands too? You know there are too many of us experienced teachers in the towns, all competing for a handful of positions and most of us will never make it to the top, we're destined to die of chalk dust! Now, Petros, it's time you stopped trying to control me and manage everything. I am NOT trying to manage you but only stating frankly that we should treat each other as equals, and put our two heads together for the benefit of our marriage. Wake up and smell the coffee,* shamwari!

One Saturday morning while she was washing the VW a young man presented himself at the gate and announced that he supplied missing car parts. After a brief discussion, he departed, returning shortly afterwards with a pair of tinted wind deflectors. Baba Lydia, who'd just woken from his Saturday snooze, found the young man trying the deflectors on the car.

'Hold it right there, you thief!' Baba Lydia snarled, grabbing at the man. 'Mai Lydia, call the police!'

The youth deftly collected his merchandise, made for the gate, leapt over it like a young antelope and vanished.

'So, Mai Lydia, you're dealing in stolen property!' Baba Lydia panted.

'The deflectors weren't even the same colour,' she snapped back.

'Same colour or not, can't you see? What these thieves strip from one car they fit on another!' You could be buying your very own missing parts.'

'Same parts or not, they're still rare parts and cheap, Baba Lydia. This is Harare, man! Wake up, *mai*!'

***

On Saturdays, after giving her extra lessons, Mai Lydia drove to baby showers, kitchen top-up parties or weddings. Suddenly, she had a flock of new friends, new clothes and new schedules. She joined parties where everyone made a weekly financial contribution that was then paid out as a 'huge' sum to each member in turn. She picked up her new friends – some with garish make-up and voluptuous bodies that threatened to burst out of their tight-fitting clothes, and voices that carried above the boom of rumba music on the car radio – who secretly pleaded with him (or were they mocking him?): 'Ah Baba Lydia, Ah Baba Lydia *kanhi nhai imi*. Your car is beeeeyutiful, *mufunge* Baba Lydia. Oh, Baba Lydia, and you're such a good husband to let your wife drive,' and Mai Lydia would grin sheepishly at her inebriated friends. But she was always home in time to prepare supper, even when he was not yet back from the shops.

One Sunday morning, searching for his red pen under the car seats, he found a half jack of brandy,

'What's this!?'

'Oh,' his wife said casually. 'Mai Nyasha had taken it from the party for her husband. She must have forgotten it in the car.'

'So you people drink strong stuff at your parties?

'Some women do.'

'And are you drinking now, Mai Lydia?'

'Me? Heavens, no.'

On Sundays she drove to her Pentecostal church (he, an avowed atheist, didn't). She would often pick up friends along the way and after the service one or two congregants would still refer admiringly to the car.

'Way to go, Mai Lydia,' the bubbly young priest chirped. 'God simply hates poverty!'

Now she had a car, no matter that the front looked damaged, many people asked for favours; with wheels she'd become indispensable to her relatives and friends. A neighbour's sick child had to be driven to hospital at night. A fellow teacher hired her to ferry a sister's wedding cake for the ceremony in Domboshawa. 'As if the car runs on water,' Baba Lydia complained, impotently. Things came to a head when she chose to drive to the Grain Marketing Board to collect empty storage bags for her rural mother, leaving Baba Lydia to use the kombis to take his ailing father for a medical check-up.

'I had to take my father to the clinic in a crowded kombi,' he grumbled bitterly.

'You didn't ask. Besides, you said you didn't want me driving your relatives around with you in the passenger seat of an old jalopy.'

'The City Council was going to cut off our water yesterday. You didn't pay the bill. I had to plead with the officer to leave it on. Besides, you're starving us. We haven't had any meat all week. '

'I told you I had to pay for the vehicle radio licence.'

'So who's paying for all the fuel?'

'Some people pay a little something.'

'Why don't you paint the Golf bright yellow like a proper taxi and call it Mai Lydia's Express, then?'

'Eh, eh, Baba Lydia, the car needs a new clutch plate, rings and so on and the only way I can raise the money is by hiring it out.'

'What plates, what rings?'

'How would you know? You don't drive.'

'Who told you that you need these things?'

'Baba Trevor. He said we need to take the car in for a thorough check-up at the VID.'

'You and that deputy of yours! Is he deputising me in my own household now? He's no longer just the new, over-zealous deputy head but a qualified mechanic, is he? So, he thinks the car needs an overhaul, does he?'

'I said *check-up*, not overhaul.'

'Check-up? Overhaul? What's the difference? Why doesn't he give you *plates* for your kitchen and a proper *ring* to solve all your problems? You think I haven't noticed how the two of you behave? Wait till my transfer comes through and I'll leave you to your pranks.'

'Eh-he! We've heard about that transfer for years now.'

'Where did you get money to buy a new battery? And the new road-licence fee? Did he pay for them? Did he?'

'Ha! Ha! No, he *didn't*.'

'Then who did?'

'Why should I tell you?'

'I *demand* to know!'

'Ask your daughter, Lydia.'

'So Lydia is part of this racket, is she? How would she get the money to fix the car when she's off sick, pregnant in Jo'burg?'

'Doesn't she have a husband with a proper job down South?'

'Aha! So now you've been going behind my back to Roderick with an empty bowl; begging from our son-in-law and making us look destitute, eh?'

'But aren't we destitute? Isn't every Zimbo? If Roderick offers to help, why should I say no?'

'He's helping you not because he wants to, but because he's embarrassed by the problems his wretched "present" has caused. You're milking him dry. I need to talk to both Roderick and Lydia. I tell you what – if he'd given you money to invest, start a poultry project, or even a flea market stall that'd have been sensible.'

'Don't you dare call Roderick, Baba Lydia, because if you do you'll only look a fool!'

***

Well, Baba Lydia did dare to call Roderick the next day. But when his son-in-law cheerily asked over the crackling mobile phone if the car was okay, he caught his breath and quickly said, 'Yes, yes,' before briefly asking about Lydia's health and that of his two small grandchildren. As wary of each other as rival bulls in a vlei, the two men skirted essentials.

Baba Lydia slunk off to the shops again like a defeated mongrel, its tail between its legs. The noise, the blaring township music, cars hooting and revving, women and men slapping hands and chatting with brash voices amidst the sputtering of frying pork and the purple whirl of braai smoke, swallowed him up into one big vibrant swell of humanity. There, he tried to forget the Mai Lydia he'd once known, the buxom, mini-clad eighteen-year-old netball sharp-shooter at teachers' college; he remembered how he had courted and eventually won her over, making her pregnant with Lydia. Now, he realised that perhaps he'd only married her because he'd made her pregnant – just as Roderick had done to his daughter. The way of all flesh. (Where had he read that?) He knew this now, some three lean decades later. Was his wife now too old for him or was he now too old for her, or were they too old for each other? Did she perhaps understand more than he did the reality of this skewed country and the mediocrity into which he'd been sluggishly ensnared. He felt like a drowning animal trapped in the branches of a dead tree while he watched his wife breaststroke downstream on the free waters of her ambition.

He saw now that with his innate fear of her drive, their romance had worn off like old paint. First had come the house (she had borrowed the deposit from her sister's husband), her degree (and the growing prospect of the post of teacher-in-charge), her driving licence; and now, with this car, he'd come unstuck.

He bought a strong beer and sat on an empty crate under a tree. A sharp-faced teenager with a purple weave and a see-through red dress jerked him from his sad reminiscences. Pulling up a crate next to him, she said, coyly, 'You're very early today, Petros. Where were you yesterday? Please buy me a Savannah Dry again, lovey.'

***

Months later, Baba Trevor's two dogs disappeared. Shortly afterwards, thieves picked the locks on his garage door, pushed the Golf out onto the lawn and stripped it. The blackout and the pre-cast wall provided them with a fine cover.

In the morning Baba Trevor woke up from an unusually deep sleep (had the vandals sprayed his bedrooms?) and found the shell of the car beached on the grass. All the wheels, lower arms, brakes and CV joints had gone and the Golf sat on four stacks of bricks. The lights had gone too. The bonnet was open and the head cylinder, alternator, filters and battery had been removed. The spare wheel, jack and toolbox were missing from the boot. The radio and speakers had been pulled out from the dashboard.

When she arrived, Mai Lydia flung herself to the ground with a keening wail like a woman arriving at a funeral. The neighbors poured in, shaking their heads and muttering 'oh's' and 'ah's' and 'so sorry, so sorry's'. Baba Trevor called the police.

Baba Lydia knelt down and covered his wife's firm abandoned calves with her Saturday-morning print cloth and held her up by the shoulders; she buried her face against his chest and wept, impotent at this new shame. Baba Lydia stroked her face and her hair, and said, '*Chinyarara*, Tambu. Hush, hush, my dear Tambu.'

She let him hold her hands in his and hug her to him and as her sobs and hiccups softened against the wall of his chest, they each somehow felt there was just a faint chance they could live through this, and that there was a little hope left for them yet.

Chioniso

Today I almost slapped her face.

Cheeky little bastard, stubborn to the core – I wonder who she takes after, her mother or me? Whatever … she has no business creating this wedge between us. She's so incredibly self-willed: determined to get whatever she wants at whatever cost, used to bulldozing her way through thick or thin with nothing but her sixteen years and her guts.

She's called Chioni, short for Chioniso – and she's my daughter, second daughter that is, but right now she is more like a sibling. When she was little she used to gather herself into my lap at funerals, and the bereaved men (male mourners always sit together) would say, 'This one is your darling for sure.' When my mother was dying of cancer, Chioni would brave the smell of wasting flesh, swing her curtains open, and ask, 'Would you like some water now, Grandma?' And when she was nine or ten she played the leading role, the Angel Gabriel, in a school nativity play and I proudly told her what a good angel she was.

Now we fight.

I hate her and I love her and I love her and hate her. She brings home reports of diligence at school and at home she's a brilliant cook – if she's in the mood. At church, she's the youth-club leader and runs the Sunday School class for infants – typically taking after her mother. Her bedroom is full of beautiful dried flowers in painted pots and she reads dreamful novels with rosy coloured covers; and I'm jealous. I exclaim, 'But you haven't read a single word I've written!'

'So,'she answers, 'you haven't bought me any clothes in two years!'

'But I spend all my money on your school fees, Chioni. Remember you go to one of the best schools in the country,' I tell her as gently as I can.

And she retorts with, 'So! What about all the beer you drink?'

This was how I felt then. Feeling consumed me. My marriage was on the rocks, and with it, all rational feelings towards the world. My position was negative, defensive. ...

I know now that she's fighting her mother's wars.

She has friends of all colours and her best friend is a white girl called Anna. Now Anna is an only child and her father is a chairman of companies and every so often Anna invites Chioniso to go camping by the lake and I say, 'Fine, Chioni, you can have all the friends you want in the world, but just remember you're black. Of course, you can go but just be sure nobody turns against you later or hurts you.'

Am I a racist, I wonder?

An uncomfortable question. What would it mean if I was?

Chioniso goes off to the lake and brings back an armload of tiger fish and startling new tastes. Suddenly the hi-fi I bought last year is too old and our house needs repainting and I talk too loudly on the phone. I can't listen to my jazz while she's doing her homework. My message on the answering machine is replaced. We need a new car. Her sheets have to be changed every day. I try to tell her off and she flees to her bedroom and bangs the door in my face just like the Cosby children on TV.

I'm helpless at her door. I encourage confrontation with my children because I think it builds intelligence. I don't want to breed monosyllabic broilers who can't fend for themselves, should anything happen to me. But who's this creature I'm breeding behind this door? Have I been too soft?

I hear pages rustling. I know she's reading her teenage Bible or some other church literature and humming her born-again tunes, just as her mother does when she's angry. I want to say, 'Once upon a time I too was a Scripture Union fan, Chioni. The Bible will disappoint you later, my daughter, or some sweet-tongued boy will ruin it for you.' I want to tell her, 'Life is a thorny, variegated plant, and not the tapestry you think it is, Chioni.' But I can't say anything. I am tongue-tied.

***

Of my three children she's probably the one most like me and perhaps that's why we fight so much. I'm a writer, she wants to be a fashion designer – we are both unrepentant artists; veritable comrades and rivals. Her mother and her two siblings are irrevocably wedded to accounts and economics. My sister Tete Tee says never in her life has she met a child so organised and yet so intractable. Chioniso seems to be in a perpetual rush; she never reads the newspapers or watches television, keeping to herself in her room. Yet when she breezes into the lounge and kneels to visitors and relatives and trickles water over their hands and offers them food with her glowing smile, like a good Shona girl, you would think all was well.

When her mother moved out and I invited our maid Sarah to move into the main house to take charge, Chioniso sobbed a storm, charging that her privacy would be violated and declaring that she would never share her bedroom with a maid. This time I did not give in. And soon afterwards I stumbled upon her open diary and – please forgive me for the impropriety, dear reader – I was horrifed to read these lines:

I simply hate him. I wish I could make him mad. I hate his scruffy clothes, his stupid accent and the embarrassing jokes he makes with my friends. He's always watching boring history and geography channels on DSTV and playing golden oldies in the lounge. I wonder who reads his books? They're always about himself, so why do people make such a fuss of him? He always goes off at night and comes back very early in the morning, often smelling of drink and cigarettes. Maybe you were right to leave him, Mom.

Then the door opened and who should burst in but Chioni? The incriminating book tumbled from my hands to the floor and I just managed to kick it under the bed out of sight. She stood in the doorway, ready to do battle for the umpteenth time.

'What are you doing in my bedroom?' her voice rose.

***

I meet Anna's father in the school car park while I am picking up Chioniso.

'Lovely daughter you have,' he winks at me. 'My daughter adores Chioni.'

I fumble with the car door. How often it happens that strangers see the best of us. Anna's father has a crop of sagacious grey hair and twinkling brown eyes. He drives an old pick-up truck, wears faded jeans and doesn't look one bit like a chairman of companies. Perhaps he's embarrassed, like me, by class. Disguises. Kindness, I reflect, like hatred, is universal and knows no colour or class or age.

Anna tosses her blonde locks away from her face, throws her bags into the back of the truck, slumps onto the seat next to her father and gives him a peck on the cheek. I'm green with envy. I have always thought daughters do, and should, love their dads!

Anna doles me a fatigued teenage smile and says, 'Hi there, Mr Chirasha. See you tomorrow, Chioni.'

Anna and Chioniso speak for embarrassingly long hours on the phone. Chioniso sleeps over at Anna's house every so often. Each time she does so, I phone Anna's father to find out if it's okay. I wonder why Chioniso never invites Anna to our house for a sleep-over? Our house is not too bad, not bad at all. They could play music. They could swim. Or just laze about in the sun. I would keep out of their way. An adventurous girl, Anna could even enjoy our food. Chioniso is an excellent cook. Perhaps she's embarrassed by our fractured lives. I wonder if she ever told Anna that her mother moved out two years ago, 'to go and pray in peace' she said, away from my alleged tantrums, without lifting a finger to provide for the children. No school fees, no uniforms, no food, no rent, no transport, no pocket money. Not a tomato, not an orange, not a sweet. Diverting her income to pay for her two-bedroomed flat and church tithes.

The weight of secrecy can be overwhelming for a teenager.

And now her friend Anna, loved and, from my point of view, pampered by her parents.

As we inch out of the car park Chioniso waves at her flock of multi-coloured classmates. We don't talk. The tension is tight in the car, like an overcharged electric circuit waiting to explode. This is probably one of the best girls' schools in the country with its terraced green fields, spacious classrooms, gyms, art rooms and a splendid theatre. The school is an idealistic cocoon, a rainbow in the wastes of this introverted country. But, of course, like every little rainbow, it reels with its own illusions, its myriad snobberies. This is an institution for company executives with fat education and transport allowances, not for poor misguided artists like me. The fees are not something one would mention to colleagues in the pub, or to relatives. But I realise now that the Chionisos and Annas of this day, by their very oblivious disregard of the wider, sneering world, are far more capable than my generation of making a fresh start, of patching things up between the races.

But was I right to send her there? Sometimes I wonder why I did not send her to some modest mission school in the mountains where she would slurp up beans and porridge, do her own laundry, sleep in a dorm and learn about endurance. Like her sister, Vonai.

***

Chioniso is as restless as ever. She's recalcitrant, deliberately disobeys my orders; challenges me on the slightest issue. I wonder if she's rebelling against her mother and me, or what she supposes we did to make her life like this. Teenagers express their dissatisfaction with their separated parents in strange ways. Or does she perhaps have a boyfriend now? Probably not. Not that I mind! A boyfriend might in fact take the attention off me. She still reads her Bible avidly, attends three church services every weekend, loves Jesus in the way only a teenager can. Now she wants a driver's licence for the simple reason that she's turned sixteen! A child of mine who wants to drive, I swear, especially a rude one, must finish school, get a job and buy and dent his or her own car on these jinxed and jaundiced roads of ours. I am not one to spoil anyone, not even myself.

There I go again. Am I a traditionalist?

What would it mean if I was?

I make an appointment with Mrs Jefferson, her headmistress, to enlist her help. A woman of great dignity and experience, she patiently hears me out, promises to speak to Chioniso, and see if she can find her a place as a boarder. She warns me, though, that there are only thirty places available for the whole school, mostly for out-of-town students and the competition is tough; that marital problems at home are no guarantee of a boarding place.

Three days later Mrs Jefferson miraculously calls me to her office and announces that she has granted Chioniso a place as a weekly boarder, for the simple reason that my daughter is one of her best students and all her teachers think highly of her.

I am elated.

So every Monday morning I drop Chioniso off at the school with her bags, and collect her on Friday afternoons. She makes new friends. She clearly loves her new life and our relationship thaws a little. Separation builds respect. We begin to talk.

At home I hold fort with Simba, Chioniso's pliant kid brother who's a second-form day scholar at an equally prestigious boys' school, and our maid Sarah. Their eldest sister, Vonai, is already at a university abroad.

Exams come and go. Chioniso passes all her thirteen O-level subjects with 'A's and 'B's.

I'm more than elated. When she shows me her results slip I rush to embrace her. She hangs limply onto my arms, her face cast embarrassingly aside but, for once, smiling. That night I take Chioniso and Simba out for dinner, to celebrate.

***

I phone Mrs Jefferson to thank her profusely and to ask about the fees for lower sixth and the cost of school uniforms.

'But she's not coming back here,' Mrs Jefferson tells me, her voice like a pail of cold water. 'She hasn't got a place any more, Mr Chirasha.'

'How's that?' I croak.

'But you withdrew her from school. Isn't she going on that Senior's Fellowship to Mexico?'

'I never suggested that,' my mind races. 'I never signed any such papers.'

'Then who did? I have the signature right here. V. L. Chirasha.'

'That's my wife!'

'Now, Mr Chirasha, I think that perhaps you and your wife need to sit down and discuss things properly before you make any decisions. Separation does not mean you have to disagree on everything. It's bad for the children, you know. For your information I got divorced from my husband twenty years ago but we still agreed and managed to send our children to college together. You're only *separated*, aren't you?'

'Yes. Yes. But can't you take Chioniso back, Mrs Jefferson? Please.'

'It's too late. We've already assigned her place to somebody else and the lower sixths are already doing their induction course. I'm afraid I can't help you this time, Mr Chirasha.'

I call my wife Vhaidha. The phone slips from my hand with a bang and I snatch it back onto my knees and redial the number with shaking fingers. My heart is choking my throat. There's no reply for a good three minutes. To be honest, I'd heard about the Senior's Fellowship months before – that Chioniso had, with her mother's encouragement, sat for the qualifying examination and passed. It's a cultural exchange programme where kids leave school for a whole year to go abroad to live with a host family eating good food, climbing mountains, swimming in the sea, relaxing, partying and pretending to learn a language. *Abrigada* this, *Abrigada* that. *Monsieur* here, *Madame* there. French fries and apple pie, please, thank you ma'am. *Guten Tag*, while their peers sweat it out at their desks back home. *Danke! Danke!* and not much to show for it afterwards. Somebody had warned me that many girls who went on the programme ended up as waitresses and call girls.

'How *dare* you do this, Vhaidha?' I demand, struggling to keep my temper in check. 'Is it really worth it?'

'If you don't have the money just say so,' Vhaidha cuts in. 'You're not working to buy an aeroplane or a train, you know. You must let your children enjoy the fruits of your labours while you're still alive.'

'Look, Vhaidha. We're not rich.'

'All you need is the airfare in forex and the medical aid. The host family will take care of everything else.'

'Do you think I would waste my precious little foreign exchange this way? Maybe I don't even have any. I won't hear of it! The kids must go to school here and then do their own globe-trotting later, on their own salaries. Look at the state of things in the country, with inflation, ever rising costs, retrenchments, diseases and death.'

'If you tested positive why don't you tell us, then?'

Vhaidha speaks in that tangential, supercilious way that sometimes makes me want to drive straight to her seventh floor office, despite the peace order imposed on me, and wring her neck right in front of her boss. She, who went to school on mangoes and peanut-butter money instructing me, a graduate of sunflowers, to take chances with our children! She, who hasn't spent a cent on the children's welfare for two years, now wants to shove the mess she has herself created into my face. Damn it, I should have listened to my colleagues, swallowed my pride and sued her for maintenance straightaway! Damn my inaction! To be honest, I think this woman wants to create situations where I have to spend, and spend, leaving very little for me to enjoy with my supposed mistresses.

***

Three weeks after the lower sixths have resumed classes Chioniso is still doing nothing. Every night I quiz her about Mexico and she says very little. She definitely knows more than she volunteers. She sits on the sofa staring away from me, her mouth shut tight while I bombard her with 'yes' or 'no' questions at which she mechanically shakes or nods her head. I smell a conspiracy. I'm angry that she can be so impervious, that I am so helpless before her whims. I learn by default and from my faithful son, Simba, that she now has a passport and is waiting for the results of her medical examination, her visa and her foreign exchange allocation from the bank. And, as everyone knows, the banks in our lovely country are dry!

Nothing can be worse than a spouse who keeps the deepest secrets to him or herself, or is unpredictable. Or who uses children as a shield in a sword-fight with his or her partner. No, reader, I try not to be too self-righteous. I have never claimed to be a proper husband, or proper father, for that matter. I know I am a very difficult person to live with. Perhaps I myself set the precedent for secrecy; was worse than Vhaidha. I realise now I was too busy working and travelling and that I delegated most of the non-material responsibilities of raising children to my wife. And now the chickens are coming home to roost on my very doorstep. And if my children have seen me come and go so freely, fly on and off aeroplanes, who am I to stop them if they get the chance to spread their wings? And what teenager does not want to do so?

Maybe Vhaidha is right.

Indecision. Indecision.

Four more weeks and still no Mexico. No visa, no forex. Chioniso is already late for the Mexico programme. And even if she gets her papers and her money, will she secure the airline bookings at such short notice? Will it work? And if the whole thing falls through how will she live with it? Will she blame her mother? Blame me? Will she run off to the streets, sell herself or commit suicide?

I ask around and discover that I can enrol her at a reputable local city college for her A-levels just in time for the next intake.

I enlist Vhaidha's mother's help, as surprisingly I'm still on good terms with her.

'Your father is right, Chioniso,' the old lady heroically lectures her granddaugher on the phone. 'Go back to school, *muzukuru*, instead of wasting time waiting for the unknown. If I hear you haven't gone back, I will come over with my clothes and blankets and camp with you at your house till you have done so.'

And so, the next day, a tearful Chioniso follows me into the office of the director of Lighthouse College, Lucia Moyo, an ex-colleague of mine at university. She calls in two assistants and they all marvel at my daughter's certificate.

'What fine results! Thirteen O-levels, all 'A's and 'B's too. What do you want to do in life, Chioniso?'

'I want to do fashion design.'

'Yes, but what do you want to do before that? For your 'A's?'

'I don't want to do 'A's.'

'Why, Chioni?'

'I don't need 'A's to do fashion design.'

'But everyone needs A-levels and a degree these days. Even a fashion designer needs accounting, marketing, management and computer skills and so on as well as the breadth and maturity advanced education affords. I presume you would still have to attend some sort of training college. Where would you want to go, Chioni?'

'France.'

'Who would pay your fees?'

'My mother.'

I press my temples with my thumbs and shake my head in anger. I don't know what to do. I definitely want to slap her face.

'Please go outside for a while, Mr Chirasha,' says Ms Moyo. 'I want to talk to Chioniso alone.'

Outside in the corridor I bang my fists against the walls. One of the male assistants notices me and smiles. 'Don't worry, Mr Chirasha. I know how you feel. You're not the only one. One white woman whacked her child in this same office for opting out after she'd paid a year's fees. Here, have a cup of tea.'

When the director calls me back into her office after some thirty minutes, Chioniso is bent over the table with her head in her hands, sobbing. Now what?

Oh my baby. I can feel the grip of her dilemma. Like one knife at her chest and another at her back.

'Chioniso has agreed to give our college a try,' Ms Moyo smiles at me. 'She can choose the subjects she likes and start classes tomorrow. Now all we have to do is fill out some forms. Okay, Chioni, stop crying now.'

***

And so Chioniso wakes up at six in the morning to bath, eat breakfast and catch a kombi to the city. At Lighthouse College she chooses to do French, computers and design. I pay a term's fees. I buy course books for her at the college and off the street; I send for others from London. I give her pocket money for lunch and for transport.

I phone the director to find out how she's doing.

'She's a great girl,' Ms Moyo says. 'She's mixing well and socialising with others. Already she has joined several clubs. Her teachers say she is coping with her classes. Don't worry, Mr Chirasha. I'll keep you posted.'

In the pubs I boast, 'I won her back. Oh yes, I won back my baby. Her sister will be a chartered accountant in two years and Chioni will do fashion design. Her brother is in third form. I told you guys. No child of mine will leave school. Children are what we work for, aren't they?'

***

Six weeks after Chioniso started attending Lighthouse College, I'm sitting in my study working on a manuscript when our maid Sarah knocks on the door.

'Come in.'

Sarah kneels politely in the open door way as she always does when she has something important to say. Something is amiss. A death in her family, perhaps, or does she need a few days off from work, a loan or a raise? But I only doubled her salary last month.

'Yes, Sarah.'

'I don't know how to tell you this, Daddy, but Chioniso was packing her trunk the whole of last week. You wouldn't know because you hardly enter our bedroom. Mhamha was phoning her every day and even came into the house twice while you were away. I couldn't tell you because she strictly warned me not to do so. I know you pay me and I'm answerable to you. Forgive me for telling you this too late, Daddy, but Mhamha came at four while you were asleep and took Chioniso to the airport. They left the security doors wide open in order for us not to hear them. Right now Chioniso is on the plane to Mexico.'

My head falls on the keys of my laptop so that the screen flickers and blackens out.

'I'm sorry, Daddy.'

I feel hollow, defeated. I creep out to the garden and my lanky shadow slouches after me, bent double. I squint at the sun. I sit at the head of the swimming pool, watching a family of herons drinking from the long neglected, algae-green water.

***

'She must have taken her alone to the airport,' my sister Tete Tee says bitterly. 'She wanted it to be an absolute secret. Neither she nor Chioniso told me about it, and I'm supposed to be the aunt.'

'But airports are serious places, Tete Tee,' I repeat, mournfully. 'The whole family, and all the close relatives should have been there to see her off.'

'And your son Simba didn't know anything about it?'

'So he claims.'

'It's Vhaidha's doing. But your children are strange, for sure.'

'You remember Elijah Madzikatire's song, *Vana tinogumbura?*'

'Yes. Elijah was right. Children break their parents' hearts. But that's only if parents allow them to do so.'

'What if anything should happen to her while she's out there?'

'Shhh. Don't talk like that. You'll give her bad luck. She's gone and you can't bring her back. She'll be all right.'

'What puzzles me is where Vhaidha got the forex if she is half as poor as she claims to be.'

'What makes you think she's poor? How do you know?'

'*I don't know!* And that's the problem.'

'Maybe she simply saved up and bought the forex from the bank or from the black market? Or she took out a soft loan from her company? Or her church donated something? Or she borrowed from her brother? Does it really matter? You men sometimes amaze me. Can't you see that she wants prove that she has brains too, and can do something on her own.'

'But surely not at a child's expense! You're right. She never called when I sent Chioniso to Lighthouse College and I knew she was up to no good. Okay. Okay. What do I do now?'

'Don't do anything, that's what. Listen, my dear brother. I know I'm twelve years your junior but I want you to listen to me. Don't phone Vhaidha and don't go to her flat. Don't ask Simba or your maid *anything*. Don't rush off to make a scene at Vhaidha's company, because if you do so she'll just tell everyone, "Look, I told you my husband is mad," and people will believe her. Don't ask Vhaidha where your daughter is. Don't even mention the name Chioniso. Just carry on as if nothing has happened. Silence beats everything.'

***

Silence.

I do as Tete Tee advises.

I do not ask Simba or Sarah anything. I do not phone or visit Vhaidha. I carry on as if nothing has happened. In my mind, Chioniso dies.

The only person I talk to about the matter is Ms Lucia Moyo, the director of Lighthouse College. She shakes my hand with her well-manicured one and says, 'I'm sorry, Mr Chirasha. You did what you could. Your daughter has made up her mind about what she wants. She's only seventeen. One day soon she will realise the chances she threw away.'

'Can I get back the deposit and the term's fees I paid to the college?'

'I'm afraid that's not possible, Mr Chirasha. The rules won't allow it. Tell me, Mr Chirasha, how long have you and your wife been married?'

'Twenty-two, twenty-three years.'

'This is between you and me. The root cause of Chioniso's problem is your relationship. Some relationships work and others simply don't and are better terminated. Maybe it's time you thought about your marriage. I know you're afraid to take the plunge but sooner or later you will have to. It's no longer a question of who's right or wrong. Of course, you, as a man, must have done something terrible to make your wife behave like this. I won't ask you about that. My ex-husband was behaving just as your wife is doing: competing with me, messing up all my efforts and trying to frustrate me. Reversed roles, you see! I put up with his inferiority complex for twelve years, until I was advised to leave him. Six years ago I left him. House and car and all. I said, *'Futsek, bye bye, hauiti shaz!'* I took our one child with me. It hurt at first but I have healed. I haven't looked back. I'm my own woman now! He lived with one woman after another, but it didn't work out. Now he wants me back but ha, ha, I won't touch that rotten twit.'

I think about Ms Moyo's words. Ms Moyo and Mrs Jefferson. Vhaidha. What make some professional women so unhappy? Why are men cruel to their wives? Why do married women do things behind their husbands' backs? Why should spouses need to compete and frustrate each other?

When Sarah is in the kitchen cooking and cleaning I go into the girls' bedroom. Chioniso's bed is neatly made up. Her dried flowers and plants are still in their vases on the sill. The textbooks I bought her, meticulously covered in plastic, are piled on the headboard. I open her wardrobe to look. The shelves are bare but for a pile of papers. Drawing sheets with stylish sketches. Blouses. Skirts. Dresses. Sandals. All autographed on the right hand corner: *Chioni Designs.*

Oh my baby!

Chioniso does not phone or write for a whole year. A career diplomat, Tete Tee ferrets details from Vhaidha and relays them to me. I learn that Chioniso arrived well, settled in with a good family and is learning Spanish and enjoying herself. I gather that at the end of the programme Chioniso wants to stay on in Mexico to do a degree in fashion design but that she might have problems extending her visa. Of course, there's the perennial problem of foreign currency! And who is going to pay her fees? Who can afford it?

***

Exactly a year later, who should call me but Vhaidha! I've already been briefed by my loyal sister and I know what she wants to say and have fully rehearsed my part.

Her voice crackles hesitantly on the phone.

'Yes?'

'I just wanted to tell you that your daughter is coming back next week,' she says.

'What daughter?'

'Chioni.'

'I don't have any daughter by that name.' I slam the phone down.

A week later I return home early from a meeting and Sarah says, 'Good evening, Daddy. Mhamha phoned and said I should cook two extra portions because she's bringing Chioniso home. I thought I should ask you first.'

'Don't open the electric gate for that woman or whoever she brings with her,' I instruct her. 'Tell her this is not a hotel and if she needs to order any meals she does so from me!'

I go out to have a drink, to collect my thoughts.

At nine I return home and Sarah reports. 'Mhamha was here with Chioniso at six and I told her what you instructed me and she said, "No problem! Chioniso can live with me at the flat!" And they drove away.'

'Good.' I proceed to my study.

***

Two months later Chioniso is milling aound her mother's flat, doing nothing.

I haven't seen her face in fourteen months.

I gather there are problems getting a new student visa and obtaining foreign currency from the bank – or raising the money in the first place. I have been adept at taking Tete Tee's advice but I'm anxious now. I hear Chioniso has visited Tete Tee twice at her office and has been to Kadoma to see an aunt – my late brother's wife. I can sense that she's reaching out, reaching back, albeit improperly, without the decorum requisite to situations like these. I feel I'm being unnecessarily ruthless, that I should swallow my pride. I call my sister to plan a new strategy.

And so one evening Tete Tee drives Chioniso to my house and escorts her into the lounge. Chioniso, slim in designer jeans and a T-shirt, sporting natural dread-locks, smiling her white Chioniso smile, shaking my hand and sitting on her favourite sofa as if she has just returned from a trip to the supermarket.

'How are you, Daddy?'

'Fine, and you?'

'Fine.'

'How was Mexico?'

'Oh, it was wonderful. I met some interesting people from all over the world and I made a lot of new friends. I learnt to speak Spanish and received a certificate in leadership skills. I also worked part-time as a waitress in a hotel.'

97

'What's it like over there?'

'Why don't you show him the pictures you brought?' Tete Tee suggests, glowingly.

Chioniso digs into her bag, brings out a fat album, and lays it at my feet. I flip through the pictures, trying not to look too interested. Beach scenes, mountains, Aztec structures, group photographs of students of various nationalities.

'I was the only black student in the group and everyone was so helpful.'

I put down the album. I'm quiet for five minutes, holding my head in my hands, wondering if I am giving the occasion the seriousness I think it deserves. Wondering why Vhaidha is not here and what will come out of this meeting without her. I can see Chioniso thinks her problems are over, but who does she think I am, Phillip Chiyangwa?

'So what are you doing now?'

'At the flat?'

'Yes.'

'I'm sewing costumes for the Malaika show and for various other people. And my friends, too.'

'So what are you planning to do with your life?'

'Maybe let's not talk about that tonight,' Tete Tee cuts in. 'Let's just say Chioni came to say hullo and to apologise for going away without saying goodbye. Right Chioni?'

Chioniso nods her head impatiently. 'I'm planning to go back to Mexico to do a degree in fashion design.'

'So it's Mexico, now, not France?'

'*Bhudhi* please, not now.'

'She must speak for herself. She's eighteen.'

'But its water under the bridge, brother.'

'Have you got a place there?'

'Yes.'

'Have you got a scholarship?'

'Not yet.'

'So how can you go without a scholarship? Does your mother have the money?'

'No. But if you pay for me, I can work part-time as a waitress and I will reimburse you fully by the time I finish the degree.'

'How many hours would have to work a day to do that?'

'Six, maybe eight.'

'You think you could work eight hours a night and go to class alert and fresh in the morning and take full-time classes?'

'I could try.'

'And you think you could pay me back with your waitress's tips? Why would you even have to punish yourself like that?'

'Look, Daddy, if you don't think you can…'

'Chioni, shut up!' Tete Tee erupts, concerned that the truce she arranged is already fraying at the edges. 'Your father never asked you to reimburse him. Did he ever ask you to pay him for the thirteen years of education he gave you? For feeding and clothing you? For even fathering you? Now listen, you two. You keep fighting like siblings. I'll have to think for you both. We can't decide anything in the absence of your mother, Chioni. I'll take you to the flat now and tonight you will sit with your mother and draw up four detailed budgets for your Mexico degree; one with your own input as a waitress and the other without – each one in Zimbabwe dollars and US dollars, for three years. I suggest the three of you meet tomorrow night at some neutral venue and decide if the Mexico idea is feasible or not and who will contribute what.'

***

And so the next evening I sit at the Wimpy waiting for my wife and child. They walk in slowly, Chioniso leading, her mother following, arms folded at her breast. Chioniso is wearing a bright yellow T-shirt and black jeans. Vhaidha is clad in a long grey winter sweater (although it's not yet cold) over a black office suit. Chioniso says casually, '*Maswera sei*, Daddy?' Vhaidha approaches me cautiously; I haven't seen her in a year. Her natural dreads are greying. She has not bothered to groom her hair and her suit is too sombre. I normally find flecks of grey in a woman's hair exciting, but her hair only looks neglected. Her skin is ashy-grey too, due to deprivation, or pious self-denial. She shakes my hand lingeringly, pursing her fleshy, unadorned lips.

'How are you?'

'Fine. How are you? Aren't you going to sit down?

Chioniso hurries to draw two unoccupied seats from the adjoining table and before they are properly seated she flings a sheaf of computer printouts on the table.

'Here, Daddy. We brought those budgets you asked for.'

I'm quiet for a minute, scratching an eyebrow. 'Hold it, Chioniso,' I say, thumbing the papers aside. 'Before we look at these we need a few explanations and apologies.'

'What explanations? What apologies?' Vhaidha retorts, scowling familiarly.

'My dear wife,' I say as slowly and calmly as I can, 'you don't just withdraw your daughter from school, a *reputable* school, whose fees you are not even paying; get her a passport and a visa, and, like a witch, sneak her off to the airport in the middle of the night, fly our daughter off to some unknown place, keep mum about her for a year, fly her back and when things get out of hand, present your husband with elaborate new budgets.'

'Now, Dad, if this is what you brought us here for...'

'I'm talking to your mother, Chioni.'

'Oh, I wish Tete Tee was here.'

'See, Chioni, your father is shouting already. See what a difficult man he is? I warned you that he would be impossible.'

'Twenty thousand US dollars a year for four years!' I exclaim as I scan the printouts. 'Do you have that kind of money, Vhaidha?'

'No.'

'Do you think I have it? Do you think even the Governor of the Reserve Bank has it? Do you earn a tenth of that?''

'You said she's your daughter. You are the father. You decide what to do about her.'

'It's your game, isn't it, to suck me dry with your grand budgets!'

'Look, Daddy, if you don't have the money, then why don't you just say so?'

'Shut up, Chioni. God! Whatever happened to the g manners we grew up with? Oh, Vhaidha, what waters did you make these children drink?'

'Well, if you two are going to sit squabbling all night I'm definitely out of here.'

'Sit down, Chioniso.'

'Bye.'

'See. You've driven her off. Now what have you got to say for yourself, Mr Chirasha?'

Vhaidha strides down to the stairs after Chioniso. I crumple the papers with one hand, fling them after her and yell. 'You know where to find me!'

'Children!' says a middle-aged couple who've been sitting next to us, listening.

'And ex-wives.' I add morosely.

'What will you have on us?' the man says. 'A beer? Come and join us for a while. Don't go off and drive in this mood. You'll kill yourself for nothing.'

***

The next morning I call Chioniso on her mother's cellphone and try to reason with her. 'I can help you, Chioniso.'

Silence.

'Listen. I can help you, baby.'

Silence. Only the rise and fall of an angry, suppressed breath.

I hang up and call Tete Tee.

'You don't learn,' my sister says. 'She doesn't care for you or for anybody in the world. She's *selfish!* The same goes for her mother. She'll know what to do with her.'

***

Dear Chioni

It's been a year and a half since I saw you and your mother at the Wimpy. You don't call or visit. I can't call you because you have no phone and your mother says she lost her hand-set or changed her number and I no longer know when your mother is telling the truth or not. I miss you, wherever you are. You hurt me deeply that day when I spotted you at the garage and tooted at you and you ran off to your mother's flat. I hear you visit Tete Tee at the office once every few

*weeks and that's okay. Remember she is, like you, a Chirasha through
and through and knows, perhaps even more than I do, the mores of the
family. I go to the shopping mall every day to do the banks and e-mail
and I keep hoping one day I'll bump into you, but it seems you and
your mother do your shopping elsewhere. Are you eating well? Did
mum buy you a new bed? Do you have a TV set? Are you reading?
Simba has DSTV now and I do wish you would drop in sometimes and
keep him company. He is in lower sixth now, doing maths, accounts
and economics and growing taller every day, like a maize stalk, and if
he passes I plan to send him to a good university in South Africa. He
can't cook properly yet, his sadza is really like porridge! Sometimes
we cook together – you should see the mess we make in the kitchen
when Sisi Sarah is away on weekends, but he's learning. Sometimes
at weekends when Sisi Sarah is not here I bring him a pizza from the
restaurant. But he's okay. On Christmas day we went to eat goat stew
and sadza remapfunde and watch Jerusarema dancers at The Krall
and he enjoyed it. How is your sewing project? Are you getting many
new customers? Good luck with the Malaika show and, of course, if
you need any help just let me know. Does Vonai phone from the South?
She last called six months ago, I think. How is she getting on with her
new job? Is she planning to come back? I hope she buys you a good
sewing machine and materials.*

*And your mother? What does she do when she is not going to work
or to church or to prayer meetings? Do you guys have any visitors at
home? Do you go to see Sekuru and Mbuya Mombe?*

*Funny, sometimes I drive around near your mother's flat and I see
a young woman in jeans walking at the side of the road and I think it's
you and I slow down. Yesterday when I was going to pick up Simba I
gave a lift to two girls from your old school. They were a year behind
you at school and are now in upper sixth. Rebecca and Maria, I think.
They said they know you and they have read my books. They said to
say hi.*

I don't know if you will reply but I would be happy to hear from you.

Love

Dad

P.S. How is your friend Anna? What is she doing now? Do you still go fishing at Kariba with her? I hope she still invites you to her house.

P.P.S. I met a woman this morning, who knows another woman whose niece is studying fashion design in South Africa. The college takes mature students with good O-levels. Are you interested? If you are I could forward you the details. It's affordable and it's close to home, you know. I can pay for you.

P.P.P.S. I don't know how to say this, but I think you and I are the artists in the family, and like all artists, we're adamant about what we desire and we want everything to happen our way, and you and I shouldn't clash so often, you know ...

P.P.P.P.S. Please reply.

Prisons on the Road

Simon fed the dog another tiny rye biscuit enquiring cheerily, 'Anybody else for one, folks?'

The huge Alsatian bitch was getting on my nerves. It kept leaping about, switching restlessly from seat to seat, licking my face and burrowing into my crotch.

There were four of us squashed in the rickety BMW sedan: three men, a woman and the dog.

It was 1990, a few days after the Berlin wall had fallen. The road from East Berlin was packed with incredulous Germans fleeing decades of communism for a foothold in the more affluent West. It was a period during which the world would heave: Gobachev's perestroika was taking root, the Soviet Union and Eastern Europe would splinter and yield to change. Africa shivered while the world waited with bated breath as the planet's best-known prisoner, Nelson Mandela, was released from jail to commence the long, tricky, final walk to free his beleaguered country from apartheid.

But here we were stuck on a four-lane highway chock-a-block with cars crawling at tortoise pace or not moving at all. Horns blared, tooted and honked rudely, impatiently, in the searing heat.

An inauspicious start.

The dog stank. We stank. The car reeked of entrapment. Outside, the air was heavy with the metallic tang of combusted fuel. We'd been on the road for twenty-six hours without stopping to bathe or eat; only getting out now and then to stretch our legs or pee on the side of the car – all prudishness had left us. We had driven from the sad slums of East Berlin, where we'd been to participate in readings and discussions, and God only knew how much longer it would be before we reached Frankfurt.

The few roadside shops had been stripped of all edibles by the migrants – all we had now was Simon's packet of rye biscuits and a case of bottled water. Vera held the dog up and kissed its nose, murmuring, 'Poor, poor Bingo. Poor girl.'

Ezeulu, who was sitting in the back between me and Esrome shoved Bingo's snout from his face and adjusted his elegant, earth-brown *bubu*, flapping it over his shoulders as if he was beating back a swarm of irksome flies. He fingered his impressive grey beard, cleared his throat and began again, irrepressibly, 'You guys think this is a traffic jam? Come to Lagos if you want to see a real jam. The roads there are something else. Of course, the concept of "the road" is so much a part of our culture and psyche. It's the very artery of our history, the route to our modern conscience. Many of our artists have used it in their works, including our very own Wole Soyinka, who has exploited it as a major symbol in his literature…'

'Great writer, Soyinka,' Simon cut in, stroking his receding hairline and tapping on the steering wheel with his small white fingers. 'Great personality, too. Last year he stayed at our flat for three nights while I was translating his papers. What a time we had of it. Remember, Vera?'

'Oh yes,' Vera beamed.

'He gave my little wife a tough time, joking and teasing her.' Simon closed the small gap between our car and the tractor ahead of us. 'But she handled it well, didn't you, my lollipop? I'd say *all* the African writers we've hosted at our flat over the years were interesting, weren't they, Vera dear? Such great humour, spirit and taste.' He rubbed a lean, pink knee through the slit in his wife's Levi's. 'But my mermaid can handle it, can't you, my little dove?'

'So you found *all* your African guests interesting?' Ezeulu remarked, brusquely. 'What do you mean by *interesting*? In the African and Arab worlds the concept might be viewed differently than it would in say French or German.'

'You understand Arabic, Eze?' I asked, more to deflect a potentially contentious point than to express surprise.

'I can both speak and write it.'

'You don't know Eze, Godfrey,' Simon laughed affably. 'Eze is fluent not only in Arabic but also French, German, and English, of course.'

'Plus Ibo, Hausa, Yoruba and Swahili,' Eze counted off his accomplishments on his fingers. 'And now I'm studying Spanish.'

'What haven't you done, Eze?' said Simon. 'You're a poet, playwright, actor, musician, novelist, professor and…'

'Critic, essayist and human rights activist.'

'Is the bag empty now or do you need a new dictionary?'

'That's from *The Lion and the Jewel*,' I interrupted. 'You know your African literature all right, Simon.'

'And how many countries have you been to, Eze?'

'Thirty-two at the last count.'

'How many languages can you speak, Godfrey?' Vera asked me kindly, turning towards us, her blonde locks brushing my face.

'Just English, my native Shona and a little Ndebele. I did Latin at high school, imagine? A useless subject. I should've done French. The only French I know is *je t'aime*.'

'That's not too bad!' Vera indulged me.

'No language is useless,' Ezeulu remonstrated. 'What's the matter with you, Godfrey? A young prize-winning author like you ought to be more forthcoming. You've a long life ahead and you should be open to the world. Keep improving yourself.'

'Poor Godfrey,' Vera winked at me and rubbed my shoulder. She turned to the fourth man in the car, Esrome, Cameroonian poet and senior civil servant, fiftyish, well preserved and unruffled in a dapper beige suit and olive tie. 'And you, Esrome?'

'Me,' Esrome began, sociably closing the book he was trying to read. 'Me I speak French, English, Cameroonian, Italian and a little Portuguese.'

'Wow!' Vera enthused. 'You Africans should organise the United Nations. Run the world.'

'Africa *used* to run the world once and might do so again in the not so distant future,' Ezeulu said. 'After all, it was the cradle of humanity. Remember one of the earliest civilisations in the world began in Egypt. If you think of Africa's vast human and strategic material resources today you'll see that the continent is poised for a great renaissance. Slavery and colonialism were of course the biggest curses on the continent...'

'And corruption and mismanagement...' Simon interjected.

'What we need first is to assert our identity, to believe in ourselves. There are some countries that were too colonised or achieved independence too late, Zimbabwe, for example,' Ezeulu struck my flank with an accusing fist.

'Southern Africans should at least speak the lingua franca of the continent, Swahili,' added Simon. 'And you should have African names and a national dress. It's ridiculous when your president turns up in the baking heat of, say, Sierra Leone, sweating in a black three-piece *woollen* suit and speaks the Queen's English. It doesn't make for progress.'

'Why are you so obsessed with progress, Simon?' Vera rejoined. 'Look what the West has done in the name of progress. We've killed the world with pollution, climate change, recession, nuclear arms...'

'World wars, holocausts...' I chipped in and immediately regretted doing so.

'Holocausts didn't only happen in Germany,' interjected Esrome. 'Look at the genocides that took place in the Americas, Australia, Russia and elsewhere.'

'What is progress?'

'Good question, Eze.'

'One day, when the developed nations have wiped themselves out with their nuclear weapons, Africa will teach the human race how to begin again.'

'Full circle, Vera,' I said. 'Isn't that interesting? Early life began in Africa and the future will begin there again.'

'But who says Africa won't be wiped out too?' Ezeulu spoke grumpily.

'I say let's have a biscuit each and give a toast to Africa,' said Simon. 'Unfortunately we don't have any wine or juice with which to do so. To Africa.'

'Yes, to Africa.'

I held up my biscuit for the toast, but Bingo snatched it from my hand, grabbing Vera's on the way as well.

***

We reached Frankfurt at two in the morning. The sprawling city was swathed in sleep. Simon found a McDonald's which was open all night and we bought burgers, chips, and sodas and feasted. Vera fed the dog half her chips and some chicken, sighing, 'I'm too tired to eat.'

'Or you want to stay slim,' I teased her.

'I keep telling her she should have been a model and not joined this wretched arts and culture business of ours,' said Simon. 'See, Godfrey? You should help Vera open a branch of the Goethe Institute in Harare so that she and I can come out to Africa to have some fun and fresh air.'

Ezeulu and Esrome slept in the two small spare bedrooms. Being the youngest of the guests, I deferred to my elders, and agreed to sleep in the large garage where I slept well enough. When I woke at ten, Esrome was splashing away, whistling jovially in the bathroom. My bladder was full, so I knocked on the door, but Esrome was taking his time, so I wandered into the small garden and relieved myself behind a withered apple tree. Bingo, watching me suspiciously from his kennel, gave a few concerned woofs.

In the lounge, Simon, wearing the same jeans and T-shirt he'd worn the day before, was already up, tapping away at his translations, a small mug of coffee beside him. I took a shower, changed my clothes and found Ezeulu arrayed in a sea-blue bubu inspecting the books which lined one wall of the huge lounge.

'I hate libraries,' I said irritably, and Simon laughed.

'Why?' Ezeulu scowled, inserting another page marker in a plump volume.

108

'Books depress me,' I continued, recklessly. 'There are billions of them in libraries and in people's homes, in stores and at exhibitions, hardly bought, borrowed, stolen or even read, while millions of aspiring writers, including me, hack away all their miserable lives trying to add another title or two to the exisiting mountains of literary rubbish.'

'You can't be serious,' Ezeulu looked at me disdainfully, as if he'd been expecting some such drivel from me so early in the morning.

'But how did you write a successful novel without reading widely?' Simon poked at his thin greying locks.

'He dreams up the ideas at night,' Ezeulu mocked. 'The dream tradition is big in literature but only the Latin Americans have perfected it.'

I remembered that two years previously, Ezeulu had been a runner-up for the prize I'd just won, which had brought me on this tour. Perhaps he was irked by my supposed success.

'And I suppose you hate readings and conferences, too,' he goaded me. 'At least this seemed evident in all our discussions last week. So why did you bother to come, young man? As for saying that African feminist writers get a better deal than their male counterparts and that we need a "Men's Movement"... well! Why talk such gibberish at an important conference? You! An educated writer! Be careful what you say, man, you'll be quoted.'

Fortunately, at that moment, Esrome breezed in on a waft of cologne, clad in a striped shirt and khaki pants.

'Now guys, here in the West each person makes his own breakfast and cleans up afterwards,' Simon told us needlessly. 'I think we've a few eggs in the fridge and some bread, coffee and tea in the cupboard.'

'I don't like breakfast so late in the morning,' responded Ezeulu.

'You'll have to wait for lunch, then.'

'Do you have cornflakes?'

'I don't think so.'

'What's for lunch?'

'Vera will make a potato and shredded beef broth. You'll like it.'

'I need to get to the post office and the pharmacy,' said Esrome.

'Vera can drive you.'

'Is she up?'

'There's a pharmacy at the end of the street and a post office twenty minutes walk away.'

'I might get lost.'

'I can get her to drive you, then. … Vera! Vera!'

The might-have-been model arrived in a flaming red nightdress, yawning sleepily.

'Can you drive Esrome to do some errands, Vera dear?'

His wife's forehead wrinkled in a tiny frown, 'But can't he walk?'

'I'll tell you who drove me around, everywhere, when I was in Cameroon,' Simon said to no one in particular, 'Esrome's wife. You'll never get a hostess like her. She always had everything that you might need. Fabulous meals too: fish, prawns, beef, chicken, goat, beans, soup, okra, cassava, and yams. She could cook fish in all sorts of different ways – stewed, fried, steamed or baked in banana leaves. Besides a gardener, she had two maids but chose to cook for us herself. We all had meals together around one big table. There were always important visitors dropping in on her household.

'And I will never forget the night Esrome took me out to a Cameroonian night club.'

'You went to an African club, Simon?' Vera bit her lower lip. 'You never told me. What did you do there?'

'What did I do there? I danced, of course.'

'With who, Simon?'

'With whom? With Cameroonian damsels.'

'But you can hardly dance, Simon!'

'Oh yes, he *could*,' Esrome hooted with laughter. I imagined Simon boogieing to rumba music, round and round in wide circles, weaving in and out, bobbing and bouncing out of step, a white amusement cheered on by a shoal of young black beauties.

Vera changed into some clothes, fetched the car keys and asked, 'You want to come with us, Godfrey?'

'He's too hungry,' said Simon. 'He's a young man and needs to feed his big bones.'

I stayed behind frying, or burning – there was very little cooking oil

– myself an egg, which I had with a plain slice of wholewheat bread and a mug of milk-less, sugar-less coffee.

Ezeulu sniffed at the unruly smells from the kitchen and continued paging through books. I sampled Simon's jazz music.

Vera and Esrome returned three hours later. After the post office and the pharmacy, Esrome had asked to be taken to the flea markets where he had acquired an amazing array of presents for his wife: bangles, necklaces, shoes, costumes and perfumes.

And no sooner were they back than he said he'd like to use the phone to call his wife. Simon blinked but said, 'Of course, Esrome. Go right ahead.'

At three o'clock Vera finally served us her famous potato and shredded beef broth with wholewheat bread; she had bought two fresh loaves, a carton of eggs, some milk and sugar on her outing with Esrome. We were all hungry and the soup was delicious. I secretly wished there had been more of it, contemplating with a little irony that we had been better fed by our not-so-well-to-do hosts in the East.

That afternoon I listened to two more CDs, went back to the garage where I took a quick nap and rehearsed my reading passages and notes. When I returned for the seven o'clock rendezvous Esrome was on the phone again, chatting away unperturbedly in his home language and Ezeulu was absorbed in half a dozen books, which were piled up in front of him. Vera had washed her face, brushed her hair and applied red lipstick. She had also changed into a short, sleeveless yellow dress, which matched her hair, and high-heeled black shoes. 'My, my!' I said.

But she was speaking to Ezeulu, 'You ought to teach me *survival* Arabic, Eze; the Middle East is such a vital part of the world today.' And when he replied, 'It all depends on what you mean by "vital part,"' she yelped with laughter.

Simon packed away his laptop, put on a creased black coat and said, 'Okay, folks. All set?'

***

At the reception there were plates of tuna sandwiches, bottles of white wine, and orange juice. Back then I was still an amateur. I did not heed the advice that one should not over-eat or drink before a performance but, concerned about the near-famine that awaited us back at the flat, I gorged myself. Vera refilled my glass. When we were summoned into the hall I took one last trip to the toilet and joined my two colleagues on the stage.

The wine had made me headstrong and, dazzled by the bright stage lights, I fell into my seat, glaring at the dark, inscrutable faces of the audience below.

Ezeulu went first. Ignoring the chairwoman's warning to punctiliously keep our presentations to ten minutes, he proceeded (perhaps because the chair was a woman, or perhaps he felt it was his duty, or both) to preface his reading with a sweeping, thirty-minute summary of the state of affairs in his nation, and on the African continent as a whole. Then he read for thirteen minutes.

I came next. Perhaps because I was the youngest and not yet as well known, the chairwoman asked me to save time and reduce my presentation to eight minutes. I plunged straight into my reading but the dramatic passage I had chosen was too long and perhaps not as provocative as it needed to be. The poetic cadence I'd hoped for did not satisfy me, especially before a German-speaking audience. Ploughing valiantly on, I hadn't reached the climax before I heard the chairwoman tapping the table with her pen. I crashed to a halt, as hesitant applause filtered up from the darkened rows below me.

Esrome stole the show. He slowly, leisurely, read five very short poems, all about love or nature and the condition of the African woman – a prudent theme in these times. His imagery was fresh, raw – different. There was loud applause and calls for more, but he judiciously packed away his books, and the chairwoman proceeded to question time.

Ezeulu fielded most of the questions, of course. Still, the discussion soon degenerated into a general diatribe on repression, inequality and the apocalyptic chaos on the black continent, and the perennial ogre of the 'language question' reared its pernicious head yet again. Cool as a mountain trout, Esrome unraveled his craft and vision. I mumbled through the one or two questions that strayed my way.

Then the chairwoman wrapped up the session and we all shook hands and posed for photos. Thankfully, it was over and I could return to my wine-bibbing. The organiser, Hans, handed us white envelopes with our honoraria. This was followed by the book-signing ceremony. To my surprise, I sold eighteen copies of my novel, which I autographed enthusiastically with brief messages. I chatted with one tall, long-black-haired lady who hovered around my desk, took my address and phone number and said she adored my smile and the sound of my voice. Vera kept refilling my wine glass.

As the crowd dispersed I saw Vera gathering up the remaining wine bottles and unopened plates of sandwiches into a large cardboard carton that she transported to the boot of their old BMW.

Back in the car, my colleagues heartily engaged in a post-mortem of the event, which was the conclusion of the tour. I stared dully out of the window into the darkening, deserted streets, feeling I had cheated, reading again and again the same passage at different gatherings on the tour.

Back at the flat, Vera put out the wine, the orange juice and the tuna sandwiches and we continued to party. The tall, long-black-haired lady, who had driven behind us in her white VW Beetle, joined us. Ezeulu detained her for a long while, explaining the history of military rule in Africa, but she eventually slipped away and came over to chat to me. She told me her name was Kristina and that she was a painter. She promised to send me her personal review of my book. I asked her why her hair was so black and long and she said she had Mediterranean roots, adding that she had been to Egypt and Algeria to trace the origins of her ancestry. She said she had an exhibition in a small town not too far away from Frankfurt and she invited us to come and see it. I told her we would try.

Simon for once abandoned his laptop, put on some highlife music and we all danced with wild abandon. Ezeulu mocked the lyrics with sudden jabbing movements; Esrome hypnotised the ladies with a slow waist dance; Simon bobbed along merrily. I aped Ezeulu, much to everyone's delight. Vera and Kristina laughed and danced with each of us in turn. Ezeulu lined us up and taught us the military strut. Kristina taught us a German folk dance. I sketched the Chimurenga routine after the Zimbabwean gurus, Thomas Mapfumo and Comrade Chinx. We danced to rumba, reggae, soul and afro jazz; Simon even had a Hugh Masekela album. Vera, legs astride, held an invisible microphone to her face, lip-syncing the song 'Stimela'.

Thanks to Vera's foresight, there was plenty of wine and food.

At last, when the early summer sky began to lighten, Vera turned down the music. I walked Kristina to her car, giddily hugged her and promised to write. When I returned, Vera was hugging Ezeulu and Esrome. I held her tightly and she kissed me swiftly on the lips. Ezeulu turned his face aside and flapped his bubu in disapproval. I decided to go to bed and left Vera clearing up while Simon, stretched out on the sofa, snored robustly and dribbled at the mouth.

***

Ezeulu and Esrome left on separate flights later that day. My flight was the following morning, so I accompanied them and Vera to the airport. We amiably signed and swapped books and contact details. Ezeulu patted my shoulder and said, 'Good luck, young man.' Truce, I thought; perhaps he and I could be friends, after all. After they'd left, Vera suggested that she and I go to a restaurant for dinner.

'What about Simon?' I asked.

'Oh, he'll be all right. There are eggs in the fridge.'

'I mean, won't he mind, you and me going out like this?'

'Why should he? He hardly ever goes out. All he does is his translations. That damned laptop is his wife. We aren't even properly married, just living together. Six years, imagine. Do people do that in Africa? You must think us strange.'

We went to a quiet meat joint at the edge of the city. We each ordered a huge T-bone steak, well-done in garlic butter, new potatoes and fresh green beans. We drank red wine and tucked happily into our food. She ate lustily, like a woman who has not had a good meal in weeks. Or who hates her kitchen.

'I want a baby but Simon won't allow me one,' she revealed with surprising frankness. 'He says he's too old to have children. He is fifty-nine and I'm only thirty-two. My time is running out. I won't be

114

thirty-two forever. He's a good man and I can't leave him. He helped to set me up at the institute. He's afraid I will leave him and so gives me all the freedom I want. Or pretends to. He thinks I flirt with all the African writers we host at the flat but he pretends not to notice. Do you think I'm a flirt?'

'I don't know.'

'Tell the truth, Godfrey. For once.'

'No, you're not.'

'Maybe I am and maybe I'm not, then. But who could live like this? Could you? It's our problem in the West. It started with the war. A whole generation of our men died at the front and half our widowed women became nuns. The women remained manning everything. That's why German women seem so aggressive. Men my age don't want to marry and settle down and have children. So the only men available for women of my age are much older than us. Do you have children, Godfrey?'

'Two little daughters.'

'And is your woman good to you?'

'So-so. We have our differences.'

'You never bought her anything. You hardly talk about her. Most African men never talk about their spouses.'

'We all have our prisons.'

'But you're lucky you can escape through travel. The key to my cell was thrown into the Arctic Sea long ago. So do you too have a mansion back home, three wives, a swimming pool, gardeners, maids, cars?'

'Not really.'

'How big is your house? Has it got a ceiling? The houses we see on TV are all made of mud and grass.'

'Not all of them.'

'Are you safe from wild animals, lions, elephants and the like?'

'Oh, yes.'

'Are you safe from malaria, diarrhoea and cholera?'

'Relatively.'

'Tell me about the food you eat. What do you have for breakfast, for instance?'

115

'The usual fare.'

'Just a poor starving arts' person like us, then?'

'Sort of.'

'I've sometimes thought of having a child with somebody else. Yes, Godfrey. Perhaps even a brown child. A brown child with a coconut skin and curly black hair would be beautiful. A brown child with intelligent, artistic genes who would not have to fuss about getting a suntan. I'd never bother the child's father about him. I'd look after him, or her, *alone.* '

She slowly licked the gravy off her thumb and said, squarely, 'If I asked you to eat the fruit, Godfrey, would you?'

'What do you mean?'

'Damn it, Godfrey, I thought you would understand but you don't. I thought you would be different from Ezeulu and Esrome and all the others but you are just another dud. Or pretend to be.' She emptied her glass and the waitress discreetly refilled it.

'Why would you compare me to the others?'

'They all think I'm easy game. A white toy to be played with and discarded. Take Ezeulu, trying to impress me with his academic achievements and erudition. Or Esrome, the sly one…'

'What did Esrome do?' I demanded, curiously.

'He thinks he's a little Frenchman. Bathing ten times a day and all that. Ha! Ha! Spending hours on my phone yap-yapping to his mistresses while openly propositioning me with perfumes and costumes. Camouflaging his flagrancy with gifts and treating me like his personal aide. He offered to arrange for me to fly to his country for supposed business just so that he could steal me from Simon. Imagine!'

'But how am I different from them?'

'I see you crave flattery. If you were a woman men would hunt you down with their poisoned phalluses. You're the biggest flirt that ever walked the face of this earth. You throw hints and then retreat. You keep your distance, play difficult to get with your goody-goody gentlemanly manners.'

She put her hand on mine and said, 'If I asked you again to eat the fruit, would you?'

'I couldn't do that to Simon,' I responded self-righteously.

'He needn't ever know. I could even visit you in Zimbabwe. I can save for the trips.'

'He's my friend and he's been a fantastic host.'

'Then *fuck* you! For a sensitive artist you've no idea at all what it is like to be a woman in need.'

We finished our dessert and the waitress came over and said, 'Will there be anything else, madam, sir?'

'No,' Vera said with sudden urgency, swishing the last of the wine in her glass. 'That will be all for tonight. And bring us the bill, please.'

Her fingers trembled and her eyelids flickered. A moment later, the waitress brought the bill, hovered in dilemma, and placed it next to Vera.

'No,' she said to the waitress, her eyes flickering, pushing the bill to me. 'The man will pay. He's a gentleman.'

I spooned up the last lonely strawberry from the dessert bowl and reached into my coat for the white envelope containing my honorarium.

***

Next morning at the airport she reached into her purse and gave me a jagged piece of stone. It wasn't in fact a stone, but a small chunk of brick and concrete with broken lines of colored graffiti.

'It's a memento from me,' she said. 'A piece of the Berlin wall to remind you that we need not build walls around ourselves. I'll write to you.'

She held me tight and I kissed her. Her small tongue swiftly slid into my mouth. Her chest heaved, and when we broke free for breath she looked up and there was a film in her eyes. I held her and kissed her again, then picked up my luggage and stepped out to the check-in desk.

'If there's anything you want me to send you, just let me know,' she called out. 'Simon and I can always arrange immigration papers for you.'

She waved slowly then turned to go. Fumbling with my bags, passport and my boarding pass, I momentarily forgot about her, but once we were high above the fat white drifting clouds where borders, cultures, manners and politics seemed pointless, even pathetic, thoughts of Vera returned to me and I felt a deep sorrow and a surprising guilt. And I knew that was not the end of her yet.

Indigenous

I'd never met him before he came to sit with Mada and me at the
Blue Stream Bar that night. In his late twenties or early thirties, he
was tall, well-built and handsome in a shiny black-striped designer
suit and pointed Italian shoes. Patting her natural black locks, Mada
commented, 'But you must know Brighton Zvenyika, Godfrey? He
reads the news on TV.'

'Oh yes, *of course*, I do,' I lied, shaking Brighton's large hand.
The truth was that I no longer watched national TV, or listened to
national radio or read national newspapers because of their blatant
one-sidedness and their sickening lack of imagination. Like nearly
everything else in the country, the media had gone to the dogs – or to
the puppies, as Mada succinctly put it.

Brighton had in tow a small slim girl with a precariously large
bust and suicidally high stiletto heels. Immediately ordering a round
of drinks, when I tried to thank him, Brighton assured me, 'Not to
worry, Mkoma Godfrey. I should thank you for the privilege of your
company. It's not every evening that one meets a famous artist.'

I inclined my head and shrugged and so he added the familiar words,
'I've read your books.'

'Which ones?' I inquired, with habitual suspicion.

'All of them,' he declared confidently.

'And which one did you like the most?' Mada asked, all innocence.

'Does a mother like one child more than the others, *maiguru*?'
Zvenyika responded slyly, playing with the loose-fitting strap of

his gold watch.

'I suppose she could, yes,' Mada replied. 'But I happen to have only one child.'

'Then *mkoma* should give you two more, *maiguru*.'

'Why don't you take off your tie, Brighton,' I said. A heavy gold necklace hung round the base of his brawny neck. It was a warm night and the place was crowded and stuffy.

I wiped my forehead and said to his petite companion, 'What's your name, *mainini*?' She sipped her brightly coloured cocktail and replied, 'Immaculata'.

'Immaculata,' Brighton gestured widely, 'Clean, spotless, pristine, pure...'

'Neat, perfect, flawless, virgin,' Mada laughed.

'This one I'll marry for sure, *maiguru*.'

'And I'd become wife number what?' Immaculata demanded, coyly wiping her upper lip.

'So, what was the main news today, Brighton?'

Brighton cleared his throat and with mock seriousness and spoke into an improvised microphone: *'Hundreds of colourful cheering women gathered at the airport to bid farewell to the Head of State and Government and Commander in Chief of the Defence Forces as he left the country on a four-day official visit to an all-weather friend, The People's Republic of China... How'z that? Or... Operation Maguta struck a new height today when the Governor of the Reserve Bank released a batch of five hundred brand-new tractors to be distributed to new A1 farmers in resettled areas. The tractors were procured through a loan provided by another all-weather friend, Iran. Or: Meanwhile, thirty-eight members of the Apostolic Faith Mission lost their lives when the bus they were travelling in collided with a truck at the forty-kilometre peg on the Harare-Mutare road...'*

Unsure if his tone was ironic, I inclined my head.

'He can recall it down it to the very last syllable.' Immaculata licked the edge of her glass with her small, pink tongue.

'So you don't have to buy newspapers, then.'

'Your TV news is so biased,' Mada interjected with her customary candour. 'Head of this, Commander of that, all the time, every day, every hour. We hardly hear about the other leaders in the so-called coalition.'

'I only read what they give me.'

'But surely you've got to *believe* what you read.'

'Not all the time. There're some things I believe more than others.'

'Like what?'

'Features, interviews with people, arts and culture.' Brighton began to pare his nails with a penknife, adding as an afterthought, 'Hey, would you like to come on my early morning weekend show?'

'To do what?'

'To talk about your books, your writing, yourself. It's a five-minute slot after the main news at six. We can drink through until four and then go straight to the studio from here.'

Mada kicked my ankle and shook her head and I kicked her back. I ordered a round of three beers and the pink cocktail, whatever it was, and the waitress returned with a swingeing bill.

'A little more publicity won't do you any harm,' Brighton drummed his fingers on the table.

'But I haven't got my books with me,' I said with feigned reluctance. 'And there's hardly any time to prepare. I mean, bathing, dressing up, and all that.'

'That won't be necessary!'

'But we're already sloshed.'

'All the better for chatting. The ideas will *flow* like the booze!'

Mada put a hand on my arm, kicked my ankle again and shook her head very slightly. I kicked her back, shrugging, and said, to Brighton, 'All right, then. Let's go for it.'

We drank and talked animatedly for the next few hours without a thought of the impending interview. Brighton was knowledgeable about current affairs and he brimmed with optimism, which was embarrassing in its evasions. Mada took him up on every issue: suppression of the media, election violence, vote-rigging, violation of human rights, the all-pervasive corruption, sanctions and the indigenisation of all the remaining arms of the economy. Brighton might as well have been an insurance agent responsible for selling a policy on a stupendous, national project.

The bar was emptying. There were only the four of us left. It was time to go. I put some money on the table. Brighton protested and folded it back into my shirt pocket.

'Next time.' He gathered up the sheaf of bills and extracted a fat wad of new banknotes from his pocket.

At 4.30 a.m. we drove to the studio. Mada and I, in my old Mazda 323 hatchback, followed behind Brighton's gleaming blue BMW. Mada and Immaculata sat in the reception lounge to watch the interview on the big screen. Brighton cheerfully introduced me to the people in the studio. I asked for the bathroom, where I washed my face, brushed back my unruly mane with Mada's afro-comb and smoothed my lips with her lip ice.

Brighton spruced himself up and put on his tie. He read the early morning news with customary relish showing no sign of having been drinking all through the night. When the cameras zoomed in on me, it was not Brighton who posed the questions, but another young journo who read from a hastily scribbled script. The questions were general and open-ended, the kind that might apply to any interviewee in any artistic field. If, however, there was scant prior preparation on his part, the young broadcaster openly sought to swing my opinion in favour of the status quo. I tried to avoid any political references and used the discussion to introduce my work. Unfortunately, however, I made one indiscreet remark about 'you young born-frees who do not fully understand the war and the intertwined nature of the past and the present', which left me with a feeling of dismay, that I had let myself down by being too forthright.

'For a person who's spent the night boozing you were generally okay,' Mada conceded. 'But your eyes were too bright and you waved your hands about too much. Anyone could tell you that were high. You introduced your work nicely, but your politics were, as usual, spineless and vague. And don't make such dismissive references to born-free's in the future.'

Immaculata was snoozing rather un-immaculately on the sofa.

Brighton shook her awake and pulled her up by the armpits. 'Up, up girl! Let's go, guys.'

She fumbled for her shoes under the sofa.

'So, where are we going now, Brighton?' I asked.

'To the garage, remember. You said you needed fuel.'

The arrow on my gauge was indeed nosing into red. All I had to my name was five kilometres' worth of fuel. We followed Brighton to an outlet on the other side of town. There was a very long line of vehicles parked beside the road waiting for the fuel to be delivered. Drivers were lounging in their cars reading newspapers, chatting, or crouching outside on the curbs, snacking on oranges or peanuts. Some of the cars looked as if they had been in the queue for a fortnight as they were coated in fine dust.

Brighton drove right past the queue to the garage exit and hooted. A security guard came out to the gate, saw him, saluted and let us through. There were several cars in the workshop but because it was Saturday. The mechanics were off-duty. A man in a white overcoat came over and greeted us, 'Morning, Mr Zvenyika. What can I do for you today, sir?'

'Give me a full tank,' said Brighton. 'And give my brother a full tank and two jerrycans to take away. I'll bring the empty cans back later.'

The man in the white coat and the guard fetched the cans from the office and filled up our two cars with a zinc funnel, and put the two full jerrycans into my boot. While they were filling up, I whispered to Brighton, 'Whose garage is this?' He smiled.

Incredulously, I grinned effusive thanks, 'Oh, thank you, thank you. I'll pay you tomorrow.'

'The fuel's on the house.'

'Oh, no, Brighton!'

'Yes, it is, *mkoma!*'

We drove back into town and Brighton pulled into a bay outside a five-star hotel and said, 'Immaculata and I are booked in here for the weekend. We're going to have a hot bath. They have electricity here. You guys want to join us for breakfast? At least they have cornflakes, eggs and bacon and fresh milk.'

'We've got to go,' said Mada, firmly. 'Our maids will be worried.'

'Very well, then. Remember to come to my farm tomorrow. You said you don't have any meat at home. I gave you the directions to the farm. I'll be there by three in the afternoon, and then I can show you the place and we can go *goch-gochering* at the bottle store in the nearby village.'

***

We had a hard time getting to the farm. The land had, of course, been repossessed, or, to put it more aptly, grabbed from its white proprietors by the new black settlers. The terrain had a derelict look. Most of the fields had not been ploughed in years; the lots that had been half-heartedly tilled by ox-drawn ploughs had thin maize stalks competing with bushes and wild elephant grass. Mud and grass huts squatted where maize, tobacco, soya beans and wheat had once thrived.

We followed Brighton's directions to a large, disused tobacco barn, but when we asked the men lolling under trees drinking scuds, they said they'd never heard of Zvenyika Haven. Then we went back down the road and stopped at a small village shop, which displayed nothing but packets of salt; they directed us further down the road, but not before Mada had bought several large packets. 'That's hoarding,' I teased her.

'You won't find this in Harare. You don't cook.'

'What do you have to use it with?'

Mada said, 'Let's just go home or you'll burn up all the fuel you were given yesterday.' But for some reason, I kept driving. We had already come a hundred kilometres and it seemed silly to give up now.

A woman carrying a huge bundle of firewood on her head eventually pointed out a line of gum trees with a dam beyond. The dam was half full and on a high ridge was a very narrow road which I carefully traversed – one wrong move and we would plunge into the water below. Sure enough, a large tobacco barn lay ahead and Brighton's BMW was parked outside it. We drew up next to the car. Beyond lay a large field of verdant wheat over which sprinklers stood in impressive rows.

There was no one around.

I played music on the car radio and we waited. About an hour later we heard the chugging noise of an engine and we saw a tractor grumbling slowly along the ridge. Brighton waved cheerfully at us. He parked the tractor, which was new, and said, 'You're here. I'm sorry I'm late.'

'We lost our way,' I told him.

'We almost went back,' said Mada. 'Where's Immaculata?'

'She doesn't much like the countryside,' responded Brighton. 'So I come out here alone. I had gone out to help plough a neighbour's field. *Kubatsirana*, you see, helping each other. That's how we survive.'

The tractor drew a row of large, shiny plough discs. Brighton was decked out in new blue overalls and work boots. He was drinking from a quart of lager and offered me an unopened one, which I shared with Mada. He gestured at the wheat and said, 'This is my place, folks.'

'Is the dam yours, too?' I asked.

'I share it with my neighbours, but I have the water rights.'

'How many acres do you have under wheat?'

'Thirty hectares.'

'How long have you "owned" the place?' Mada muttered. 'Have you got the papers for it?'

Brighton shrugged and said, 'See, you guys are sitting on your bums and losing out. You too ought to have a piece of the national cake, *mkoma*. Our land is our right and that's what we fought for. The land is fertile with the blood of the comrades who fell during the war. It's time to reclaim it and our other resources. Indigenisation! Indigenisation! That's our new refrain. If you're interested, *mkoma*, I could introduce you to a person who could arrange for you to have a place like this. Easily! You're a national hero in your own way, you know, like Oliver Mtukudzi, Stella Chiweshe, Dominic Benhura and others.' His voice tailed away.

'We can't *all* be farmers,' said Mada, petulantly. 'Unless you mean *briefcase* farmers. Real farming is a calling, not a pastime for every Tom, Dick and Harry. It requires knowledge. Did you find the wheat already planted when you took over?'

'You ask too many questions, *maiguru*. Jump into my car. I'll show you around.'

He drove us round the wheat field and into a patch of forest, then to a large vlei. 'Our forefathers used to own this,' he said. 'Long before the days of colonialism. We're only taking back what belongs to us. I plan to start a dairy herd here soon.'

'Do you have the capital?' I asked.

'I can get a loan at the bank.'

'Have you got collateral?'

'There are new indigenous banks that understand.'

'But most of those banks have already collapsed.'

In the middle of the forest we reached the sprawling white farmhouse. The rooms were empty and there were roaches everywhere. The white paint had faded and peeled. In the large lounge, there were new ashes in the fireplace. The mantelpiece was stained with recent smoke. Some of the windowpanes had cracked.

'I plan to repaint and furnish the house with the proceeds from the wheat,' Brighton enthused.

Two men slouched out of one of the bedrooms and Brighton said, 'This is Kefas and this is Ananias. They stayed behind when I took over after the other workers left. They help with the goats.'

'How big is your workforce?' I asked.

'Right now I have a few hands. But I plan to build on it when I start the dairy herd.'

Behind the house was a large improvised goat pen built of wooden poles and grass thatch. At a signal from Brighton, Kefas opened the wooden door to the pen and we looked inside. There were perhaps eighty goats in the pen. Brighton said, 'How many do you want?'

I looked at Mada and for once, she replied eagerly, 'Two each.' I nodded.

'The meat will last you months. You can always come back for more.'

We chose the four biggest beasts and the men quickly slaughtered them, strung them up, skinned and gutted them.

'I have problems with thieves,' said Brighton. 'I'm waiting for a

126

gun permit for my guards.'

We gave two goat heads to the men to thank them for preparing the meat. Mada wanted to offer one, but I insisted on two, though I knew her taste for exotic stews: how she would stuff the heads with tomatoes, onions and peppers and boil them for hours until they became soft and delectable.

I handed Brighton money for the goats and he shook his head and said, 'Okay. If you insist, give half of it to Kefas and Ananias.' I gave the money to the two workers. As they loaded the meat into the boot I heard Brighton saying to them, in low tones, 'That's part payment for the last three months, eh, guys.'

It was too late for us to go *goch-gochering*, braiing meat and drinking, at the local bottle store; it was a long way back to the city and Brighton said he had to stay behind to chat to the neighboring farmers about setting up a roster for the tractor. We loaded the meat into my car and we left him there and drove carefully back down the narrow ridge towards the main road.

***

After that Brighton would come and sit with us whenever he saw us at the pub. Sometimes Immaculata was with him, and sometimes not. Often he would walk in, greet us, have one or two drinks and then leave on 'business'. He always seemed to be rushing off somewhere to read the news, visit the farm or the garage, or meet with important people; there was talk of a boutique and a hair salon. I wondered if he ever slept and, if he did, what he dreamt of. Slowly, he took the liberty of hugging Mada closely and kissing her on the cheek. At first we didn't mind him but later Mada would crossly slap his hands off and I'd look aside with a small cough. He would laugh and then edge away after embracing me too and secretly instructing the waitress to give us more drinks.

'Do you think he's gay?' Mada asked me.

'I don't think so,'

'Then what does he want?'

'We'll soon see.'

One day he was exceptionally happy and drunk. He called me over to his side and showed me something in his hand: three pieces of rough brown stone, not particularly bright, each about the size of a small thumb.

'What are those?' I asked.

'Can't you see, *mkoma*?' he exclaimed. 'Stones, man. Diamonds. Fresh from Chiadzwa. And this is nothing, *mkoma*. Some of our chefs purchase bags of them. Beautiful country, ours. Why do you think they called it the House of Stones?'

He laughed uncontrollably. I glanced at Immaculata and she winked knowingly.

'We don't want to visit you starving on sadza and beans in Chikurubi Maximum, *babamnini*,' I warned.

'Me starve in prison? You don't know me. You don't know us. We are free as *nyamavhuvhu*, August winds. We're everywhere. We've infiltrated every strata of society – schools, shops, churches and hospitals. No one can touch us. We keep dissenters in place and are generously rewarded for it. The sky is our limit. We first took the farms, now we're setting our eyes on the mines. Then, finally, we'll seize the industries and the banks.'

'That will be the end of everything,' groaned Mada. 'Amen.'

'Come outside, *mkoma*,' he said to me. 'There's something I want to show you.'

He dragged me by the arm to the car park and opened one side of his jacket. There was a gun wedged in his belt.

'Where did you get that?'

'Where did I get *this*? Where do you think I work? I can deal with problems quick and easy, and nobody will ask any questions. I have friends in high places. Tell me if anybody gives you any trouble. I'm here to protect you, *mkoma*.'

'Why would I need protection?'

'You and your books. You've no idea who's after your head.'

'Does Immaculata know about this?'

'Of course not.'

'I won't tell Mada,' I whispered, as we went back in. But, of course, I told her as soon as we were alone.

'He's probably a CIO agent,' reflected Mada. 'I've always suspected as much.'

'What about the BMW and the garage and the farm? Why does he take the menial job of newsreader on TV if he's so well off?'

***

'I'm expanding the operations at the garage,' he told me expansively, one night. 'I'm starting a new car sales department. I'll be importing the latest models: posh vehicles and good used ones. I want you to be on my board of directors.'

'Me, why? I don't know *anything* about business.'

'That's exactly why I want you on the board. Through your supposed ignorance you'd ask the right questions that would keep the board focused. Your writing and organisational skills would be invaluable. As a respected public figure, you would add enormous credibility to my board.'

'I'm too busy.'

'It will only take a few hours of your time each month. And you'll get paid handsomely for it. Who knows, you might end up as a shareholder.'

'Who's financing this?'

'It's a small consortium, but I'm the MD.'

'Who else have you got on the board?'

'Captains of commerce and industry. A hotelier. A lawyer, a civic leader. You.'

'Who are the others?'

'I can only reveal their names once you give your consent. Why don't you come to the garage some time soon and see what I've set up. My attendants will show you around.'

Out of curiosity, I drove to the garage the next afternoon. Just as Brighton had said, there was a new sales department, brazenly advertised, with a small fleet of brand new and good, used models. I pretended I wanted to buy a car and the squint-eyed attendant let me look around.

'Who owns this garage?' I eventually asked.

'Why would you want to know?'

'Who's Brighton Zvenyika here?'

'Do you want to buy a car or not?'

'He referred me to this place. Is he a salesman here?'

'Why you are you poking your nose into other people's affairs? All I know is he's our boss.'

That evening Brighton called me, 'So, did you check out the place?'

'I did.'

'What do you think?'

'I don't really think I can do it.'

'Think again. I can show you all the papers. Everything's in order. All the other prospective members have said yes. I can reveal their names to you, if that will help you decide. I'm waiting for you.'

The following morning he called me again and said, 'Have you changed your mind?'

I said, 'No.'

'You have no business acumen at all, *mkoma*.' He clicked his tongue with sudden, bitter contempt. 'You want to die poor with those wretched little books of yours. Who do you think reads them, anyway? If it wasn't for the little attention we media people give you now and then you'd be a nobody. Look at me. I'm a businessman, a farmer, an entrepreneur and I'm only thirty. I plan to go a long way, and I will. You probably wonder why I read the news on TV. I get paid a pittance for it. But it helps me *network*. People see my face and hear my voice and they know there is a Brighton Zvenyika out there. I get to meet and rub shoulders with personalities that matter in the country. As for you...'

***

After that, he stopped sitting with us and buying us beers. Sometimes he would just nod and move into a corner with Immaculata, or some new female acquisition.

'Good riddance!' Mada was, as usual, very straightforward. 'He did us all those favours just so that he could use you. I think he's nothing but a front for some political chef. Don't get yourself involved with those crooks.'

'I've never sponged on any one.'

I was not annoyed by Brighton's condemnation. I felt sorry for his sense of hurt, though I was guilty in that I had perhaps abused his generosity and somehow misled him.

Essentially, I concluded, he was a well-meaning young man struggling with an irrepressible ambition. Like all young go-getters, he wanted to leapfrog over the past, and the present, and launch himself into a glorious future, at whatever cost. I had often warned him that he should slow down and take things easy, or he would suffer burn-out. Where would he be at forty-five?

Among the proliferating legion of latter-day 'entrepreneurs', I knew a businessman not much younger than me who'd started out this way, ruthlessly reaping the fruits of indigenisation, cutting all corners, lying and cheating till he could openly boast that he owned a quarter of the land in the capital. He had strings of businesses, mansions with scores of bedrooms, several wives and tribes of children. His file at the income tax office, it was said, had been permanently 'lost'. But he never looked well; regular migraines and other ailments provided a staple accompaniment to his 'success'.

It later turned out that Immaculata was fleecing Brighton, but that only boosted his ego. The more he lavished on her, the prouder he felt. He not only took her out, but bought her clothes and groceries, furnished and paid the rent on her flat and satisfied her every other whim. One day Mada and I chose to go to a different bar and we caught sight of Immaculata sitting there, fawning over an elderly, bald-headed man smoking a pipe. She glanced at us, pleading with us not to tell, and we moved to a corner. But, of course, Brighton had hatchlings waiting in other nests for him as well. Sometimes we caught sight of them, always at a different bar, but to avoid confrontation or embarrassment, we always left.

***

I did not see him for weeks after his car sales outfit opened. I had very nearly closed this chapter in my life and I imagined he had too and moved on to classier haunts with each new venture.

One day I spotted him at a traffic intersection. He was driving a brand-new white Mercedes Benz, its seats still wrapped in plastic, a temporary number plate stuck on the back window. He was wearing a beige suit and red tie and smoking a large cigar.

When our eyes met he hooted loudly and motioned with his hand at his ear as if to say, 'Call me soon!' I thought he looked harried.

Days later, Immaculata entered our pub alone. She joined Mada and me and asked us to buy her a drink. Her skin was pale and she'd lost weight. The weave on her head was dull and tatty. There were half-healed cuts on her forehead and cheeks. Her eyes swivelled hungrily round the pub.

Mada said, 'Where's Brighton?'

'Haven't seen him in weeks,' Immaculata replied. 'He took me for a long ride, that one. For months he had not paid rent on the flat, though he told me he had, and they kicked me out and attached all the furniture. I moved out to Chi-town to stay with my sister. But still Brighton's wife sent a gang of thugs to beat me up.'

'Shame.'

'So he's married, then?' I said.

'What did you think?' Mada frowned.

'Two ten-year-old twin girls. The four of them squashed into two small rooms in Highfields. He never told me. Things have not been smooth for me, I tell you. And life hasn't gone well for Brighton, either. Because of the ZESA power cuts, the sprinklers at his farm didn't work, the wheat dried up and there was nothing to harvest. The dairy project never took off. Because he wasn't paying his workers, they connived with thieves and went off with all his goats and the tractor.'

'Whose farm *is* that?'

'I don't know.'

'Is the garage his?'

'How would Immaculata know?'

'As if that was not enough, he had a terrible accident three days ago. I heard he was driving a brand-new Benz.'

'I saw him in it.'

'He ran head on into a stationary twin-cab and broke several ribs. The car was a write-off. Right now, he's in hospital, his ribs pinned together with bits of metal. He hadn't insured the car and the owner of the twin cab is claiming damages. *And* something was not right with the papers for the Benz. His car sales outfit is ruined.'

'Poor Brighton.'

'Funny, the hand of fate,' said Mada. 'They say, in Shona, "what is not yours is not yours".'

***

He creeps into the bar. His chocolate suit hangs on his shoulders as if on a scarecrow. His navy tie is displaced. His face is gaunt. He steals into his favourite corner and hauls himself slowly onto a seat. He yawns with pain. He orders a beer. His hands shake as he raises the bottle to his mouth. The foam coats his unshaved chin. He winces at the waitress. Mada and I approach him cautiously. He smiles weakly at us. He tilts a shoulder slightly and opens his jacket, undoes the buttons of his shirt. He guides my hand into his shirt. I feel the bandages, the hard bits of metal and bone beneath. I smell the odour of disinfectant. Our faces are pregnant with impotent questions. I feel guilty, that I am somehow a part of the cause of his injuries, his fate. That it is really me stitched up gawkily inside his suit, slowly giving off that slow sure odour. Me, a fellow indigenous of sorts.

Mada fidgets with her drink. He lights a cigar and waves the smoke out of his face, as if flicking our sympathy away.

'They couldn't keep me in that bloody stinking hospital a day longer,' he says, by and by, gulping his beer. 'I discharged myself.'

He pulls on his cigar and coughs, 'Get me another quart of lager, Godfrey. You owe me a tonne of them, and it's about time, too, man! And when we're done you'll drive me home in your car to Highfields to my wife and kids. God, I need rest.'

Last Laugh

At the gate she nearly collided with a cat strapped up in a white bandolier. Two scrawny dogs were alternately courting and kissing with their snouts, or sniffing in the half-light for condoms among food scraps, waste paper and garbage. Trying to make love at the foot of a hill of demolished brick and mortar, they were eager to beat the curfew of daybreak, after which children and grown men would surely – spitting with half-savage glee – kick them to separate them from their lustful union, or curse them away with stones.

As if the human race never made love! Or, better put, as if the human race never engaged in sex. She imagined the National Sports Stadium packed with people all rising and shouting 'Gooooal!' Where did they all come from? All those thousands of people, those zillions of humanoids swarming the streets of the world, if not from the same seedy, sticky, smelly depths of the human anatomy? How much sniffing, moaning, grunting and coming had gone into their individual making? How much gasping and clasping?

Funny, she thought, how in these cramped, sleep-suffused rooms couples were nakedly, heatedly, disentangling from each other with nothing and no one to whip or kick them apart but the stark fact of their disparate lives; groping and fumbling in dazed hordes to face the new day. Outside bathroom doors, voices in the frantic queues were urging, 'Hurry up in there, Auntie! This is not a maternity ward. Are you giving birth to quads or skinning a pig or what?'

But now, with her husband having half deserted her for Botswana (to look for a job, so he said) and her two children packed off to her mother in her village, (cheaper schools, simpler meals, no transport fares and more room to play in – plus God's fresh country air, of course) all she'd done over the last three years was work and work every day to fend for her family and her ageing mother.

Half-buried in the rubble, a sign read: PRAIVET PECKING, KEEP OFF THE LONE PRIZ, though there was hardly a blade of grass in sight. Down the street, in a chicken-run as yet un-touched by the demolition crews, a lone rooster crowed, belatedly, '*Kukurigo-rigo*'. From behind a hedge, a tramp yelled, '*Rigo, rigo* your mother's! We're up already, idiot.' Spotting her, the man hastily buttoned up his trousers, straightened his cap, stood to attention and said, 'Sorry, Mai George. I didn't hear you coming. Eh, eh, excuse the language. Please do proceed.'

At the Home Industries Centre, or what remained of it, among gaping walls, smashed windows, mangled door-frames and torn roofs, a few surviving signs brazenly announced:

MAI IVY, ENTER-NATIONAL 'MAZONDO' WITH FULL
(MUTI) FOR TYRED BACKS
FRESH EGGS LAID HERE WHILE YOU WATCH
KWALFIED HARE-DRESSER, FRY YOUR HEAD QUICK!
CAR-PANT-RY – ODROBS, SOLFAS, CHAIRS RAPED HERE
GOBLINS BOUGHT AND SOLD INSIDE – ALL SYZES AND
AIGES

Under the eggs' sign an enterprising customer had scribbled, 'Have you tried to sing to the hens?' Under the goblins' advertisement another had added, 'Do you also sell Maenza lightning from Mutare?'

There was already a sizeable queue at the bus stop. A kombi bursting with human cargo squelched to a halt to pick up a few frenzied passengers then idled, swaying like the back of an elephant. An elderly couple scrambled in. Mai George squeezed in past the red-eyed, wild-haired *hwindi*. The bald man sitting next to her said, to no one in particular, 'Gehena is better, don't you think – there you don't have to spend any money on firewood.' Another man two seats ahead cut in, 'Yes, but there'll be a lot of gnashing of teeth.'

A toothless old woman blabbered, 'Thath doesnth conthern me.'

'Not so fast, *gogo*,' chirped the bald man. 'Everyone without teeth will be provided with a brand new set. And there won't be any Razaro to bring a drop of water.'

'No sacrilege meant,' coughed yet another, 'but I think hell is where all the real people will congregate.'

The *hwindi* clutched at the sheaf of notes between his lips, like a cat grabbing a flaccid mouse, his body rocking with the jerking bus. The fare had gone up again – a daily event. The young man swung into action, 'Heaven or hell, pay up, parents. The fare is like a snake – it has no reverse gear,' as he stuffed the notes into a paper bag.

In the kombi the speakers were turned up to maximum volume. Hosiah Chipanga's blaring voice was counselling his fans in Shona:

BEER IS OK – IT DOESN'T INTOXICATE TEE-TOTALLERS

THE PUB IS OK – IT NEVER VISITS YOUR HOME

KANA JERE RAKANAKA HARIMBO KUSUNGI ...

As if in competition, another kombi passed by, in the opposite direction, with Xtra Large chanting:

(I LOVE YOU, I LOVE YOU. COME STAY WITH ME AT

OUR HOUSE)

MY FATHER HAS A MACHINE WHICH BENDS BANANAS

AND *VANE KAMWE KAMUSHINA KANOITA ADD VANA*

VEMAZAI MUMAKANDA ACHO

(I LOVE YOU SO MUCH) I COULD CHEW THE TAR OFF

THE ASPHALT ROADS

AND MAKE THE D.D.F. COMPLAIN

***

At the supermarket her favourite butcher winked at her and said, 'Meat has gone up again, Mai George. Before they year is out, we'll be stewing each other. *Zvatsuro nagudo. Sekuru huyai tibikane. Sekuru ndatsva ndatsva.* Human goulash, *a la carte*. Or, as my grandfather used to say, back in the days of loincloths, "We will dine on *dhaka nejecha.*"'

She ordered cow and pig trotters, offal, ration beef, fish, *madora* and a medium-sized bag of mealie-meal. At the till, the operator, who was one of her faithful lunchtime customers, said, 'Mai George, have you heard about the farmer who bought wheelchairs for his pigs?'

'Why?' she inquired dryly.

'Because his wife loves pigs' trotters.'

'Oh.' Mai George had heard all the jokes before. People loved to laugh and hold the world at bay.

'And did you hear about the evil – sorry – civil servant who tried to organise a demonstration against the Governor of the Reserve Bank?'

'Why?'

'He was so broke he wanted the governor to reinstate the three zeros on the new currency.'

'Really?'

Did you ...? Did you ...? Did you? Mai George smiled obligingly, loaded her purchases into an old sugar bag and lugged them to her open air 'kitchen' under a muunga tree at the back of the industrial sites. She retrieved her kitchenware from a friendly garage and got her pinewood fires going. For hours she was boiling, stewing, frying, stirring and ladling.

Her customers were a pretty mixed lot, most of them from the surrounding industrial zones – motor mechanics, glaziers, garage attendants, electricians, cobblers, plumbers (did the latter ever thoroughly wash their hands, she wondered; was it possible to scrape out the grit from underneath their fingernails, to rinse the dirt out of their lives?) There was a sprinkling of kombi drivers, secretaries, several police constables and one or two teachers. She was an excellent cook; her food was fresh, hot and wholesome and she was brisk and good-tempered. Her portions were generous. She even gave meals on credit to her more regular clients.

Business was unbelievably good, great, in fact, as long as the police did not raid her. And she could always bribe an officer or two with her servings. She knew you could rarely go wrong with the human stomach. Digging into her mouth-watering pots, fishing into her quivering blouse for change or rummaging in her capacious bag for a notebook or a pen, she was convinced that she could stave off destitution. Once a customer had remarked, 'Surely Mai George, you are now earning enough to pay five teachers every month' And she had replied, 'Ha! Ha!' (Why do people so cruelly use teaching – once a revered profession, as the yardstick for poverty.) Or, 'Come on, Mai George, you definitely only hear about "hunger" at your next doors!'

But for how long would she be safe? When would Murambatsvina, the urban 'cleansing' project, catch up with her?

*****

At one o'clock the customers surge down to Mai George's kitchen. Lips parched and eyes ablaze with hunger. Temples sweating. Chests bristling with immodest hairs beneath exhausted industrial overalls, displaced ties; a shamelessly un-helmeted police corporal's head there, manicured secretarial feet for a sweet while released from vengeful high heels, the odd whiff of cheap perfume gone secretly stale under office desks, a pair of hopeful passers-by. Bodies pushing, calloused work hands with square thumbs thrusting out plates, humbled backs bent forward, throats bobbing, hungry fingers pointing, eyes digging and turning in the gravy, throats already slurping, swallowing ahead of their turn. With her bright apron and ladles, Mai George swivels over her pots, a benevolent matron of meals, immune to their relentless jests as each customer tries to outdo the other with *double entendre*, the unexpected and the saucy.

Mai George was a modest woman, she smiled politely when required, but she did not openly engage with her customers' repartee. Joking, like breathing, made people's lives easier. She knew this, even when she herself was not often amused. She secretly felt that humour never really worked unless the jokes were attached to specific personalities and situations.

'Honour ladies.'

'Not since they chose to go to the Beijing Conference.'

'Who says we want to be honoured? Who says we even want to be called "ladies"? Honour thy father and mother, twit.'

'Eh, eh, snotty face, get out of my way.'

'Oxygen dealer. Your nose is bad for the ozone layer.'

'Greedy Goriati.'

'Dinky David. Where's your sling today?'

'Knife head.'

'Scud chest.'

'Owl face.'

'*Chipendani* legs.'

'Knock knees!'

'Fanta face. Coca-Cola legs.'

'AIDS haircut.'

'Zimbo Zombie Zim.'

'*Mubvakure – kumusha kunosvikwa mai varoodzwa.* Home so far away that when you get there you'll find your mother remarried!'

'Mother who climbs trees!'

'No, rides order bicycles.'

'That's why you worship your ancestral spirits with Scud beer!'

'You and your gumboot dances.'

'Stinking tribalist! What about *Chembere yokwa Chivi*, that old woman from your village who boiled granite rocks till they were soft enough to eat?'

'But who gave you education – headmasters, nurses, army generals?'

'And who gave you standard Shona?'

'Standard 1, Standard 2, Benny and Betty, day by day. Filthy *skuz apo's*. *"Batai zvikwama vabereki!"* That's all you know. Go back to Mbare, boy.'

'Did you hear that The Dairy Company has closed down in Masvingo province, and that you will soon have to ask lactating mothers to squirt their milk into your tea?'

'Yuk! Did you hear there is now only one dentist left in Chitungwiza, and that *n'angas* and *mapostori* are making a killing treating people? I'm going to join ZINATHA and become a rich herbalist.'

'Or better still, *mupostori* –

Kuti svetu kumutsetse we shuga

Kuti svetu kumutsetse we nyama'

'Don't mock other people's churches, guys. What about your *Wapusa Wapusa* sect – grabbing each other's wives as soon as they

139

switch off the lights to "pray"?'

'Or the pastors of these rabid Pentecostals, marrying their own sisters' daughters or impregnating under-age celebrants?'

'Okay. Okay. Point taken, sir.'

'What's wrong with you today, Clopas? Your face is so funny it would make a skulking thief laugh.'

'What about yours? It's so ugly, children will see it in nightmares.'

'And you, my dear sir, are as horrible as a hyena.'

'Civet cat.'

'You're so poor you cook your sadza in a tea-pot.'

'And you, madam, wash your pretty face in a plate.'

'Thank you very well, February. You should do something about your clothes, man, all this mix and mis-match and layers. If a donkey came by it would munch you up mistaking you for a cabbage.'

'Fish-mouth, I'm in a hurry. Can I liberate this plate?'

'Eh, eh comrade, I thought we had long finished with this liberation business. Stay away from that plate.'

'Yes, stay away.'

'Stay away from stay-aways.'

'Off with you! You think this is sadza prepared by City Council labourers, ready in two minutes and stiff like a Shangaan staple.'

'Say, Mai George, are your chickens broilers, off-layers, good country road-runners or border jumpers?'

'Or stray ngozi fowls with curses strapped up to their necks which drive their slaughterers insane?'

'Shut up and eat quietly, Never. Your sandpaper belly can't tell the difference between a seasoned road-runner and a ngozi fowl. And besides, you are mad enough already.'

'Don't jump the queue, Petros. You didn't buy nappies for Baby Jesus.'

'Now that you've finished taking over white farms, whose bedroom are you invading tonight, comrade?'

'I'm not a comrade.'

'Or are you sleeping all night in the so-called petrol queues – tucked up in your small house's warm arms again, while some smart street kid, no, street *father*, dipsticks your wife?'

'Come on.'

'You're not a comrade? What's your real name, then? Donewell? Golden? Takesure? Toffee? Two-Boy? Obvious? Putmore? Forget? Definite?'

'Try Again!'

'No, he's not Try Again. He's Doughnut.'

'You would think this country has run out of names, sometimes. No water, no petrol, no electricity, no cooking oil, no bread, no soap and now no names.'

'Just like Zimbabwe-Rhodesia. Who was the son and who was the mother of that wretched colony?'

'And who was the grandmother?'

'*Southern* Rhodesia.'

'Reminds me of my old, half-blind granny who used to "read" the newspaper upside-down and swear, at every photograph, *"Iye Dhagirasi Smisi watinetsa zveshuwa."* Ian Douglas Smith has given us hell, for sure.'

'Oh, that goat-eyed bastard.'

'But who is not a bastard these days? At least when Goat-Eyed was in charge, we did not starve and there was a semblance of order.'

'Shut up, Bornfree. You never got expelled from school or detonated a landmine.'

'Hey guys, I know five brothers called Scud, Shoe-Shine, Shame, Anus and Progress.'

'Give us women's names too. Gender, man, Gender!'

'Is that your name, madam? Gender? Be careful how you pronounce that word in Shona.'

'Eh, eh, Christmas, watch your mouth. We have decent women here. Wives of husbands.'

'But I'm also a husband of a wife. *Ndiri murume wemunhu veduwe!*'

'Mai George is *blushing*. Look at her cheeks. My poor *ambuya*. Can we change the subject?'

'Okay. Have you registered to vote, Bornfree?'

'I lost my Grade 5 school report.'

'What moron told you they need that at the registrar's office?'

'My aunt.'

'While we are at that, did you hear about the chef who said at a rally, "This time we want to win all the erections"?'

'What about the chef who never took the trouble to study the speeches his aides wrote for him and once when he reached the end, read straight on, "Sorry, *chef*, I have to queue for cooking oil. Now you're on your own! Good luck, sir."'

'And I bet you never heard of the venerable chief who went to America and on meeting his first African-American grabbed his hand and gasped, "Aren't you old Zebediah's mother-in-law's cousin's nephew's niece from Nembudzia?"'

'*Aiwa!* What of the two songs by our two famous musicians about old age and education which two chefs sarcastically bandied about at each other? *"Dai Ndakadzidza ..."*

"Bvuma wachembera!"

'Or, "We looked at Mai Tsvari's behind and it was okay. We looked at her front and it was okay. So we inserted her on this seat ..."'

'*Iwe. Iwe*, Bornfree, enough. We don't want you locked up. Right, Corporal Weeds?'

'It's a free country.'

'At least there is free food and accommodation in the jail.'

'Beans, salt, lice and lustful inmates. You'll come out pregnant with *kwashiorkor*.'

'Or stick-lean with AIDS.'

'Don't worry. With AIDS, all this diaspora business, cross-border trade and professional black people going off to wipe up old white folks' bums in London or to drive battered taxis in "Harare South", the country will soon be half empty and nobody will want for jobs or accommodation any more.'

'Only you will be paid in soap and beans and salt, like in old times. *Chikafu ndodha* – each man for himself.'

'And at the rate Murambatsvina is smashing down shacks you will lodge in dogs' kennels, with Kutu, Racer, Shumba or Boxer.'

'Out of my way, Shallot. Stop acting as if you dressed mother elephant in a bikini.'

'Eat! Eat! Eat all you can now, folks. *Idyai mughute*. Glut yourselves on Mai George's cuisine, your excellencies, highnesses, mediumnesses and lownesses, ladies and gentlemen, comrades and friends. If you could reverse evolution you would maybe develop humps like camels in which to store food for future use. By this time next year you will be munching air-pies, sipping toilet-flavoured Mukuvisi River H^2O and soaking up vitamin-rich sunshine for lunch. And you will all be stepfathers and stepmothers.'

'What's that?'

'You'll be using your legs, silly, instead of these expensive and hazardous kombis. Stepping off to and from work. Left, right, left, right. R1, R2.'

'Regiment 1, Regiment 2?'

'No, Renault 1, Renault 2, silly.'

'Good thing is, there will be fewer people suffering from overweight, or high blood pressure.'

'Hand over that mug, Miss Funerals. Surely I won't get AIDS from it.'

'Who's Miss Funerals?'

'You.'

'How's that?'

'Forgot how we met at Old Mambara's wake last weekend? Do you want me to tell this august assembly that you never miss a funeral? You, Madam Bowsticks, get by on funerals. Whenever you find one you announce yourself noisily, flinging yourself in the dust and howling up a storm like the appointed chief mourner. Then, eventually settling down, you wolf down a generous plate of sadza, beef and cabbage, sit back, a warm Coke in each hand, then cleaning your teeth with a matchstick, you calmly ask, "Who's died this time, folks?"'

'Ha! Ha! I'll get you. You think you're smart, don't you, Privilege? You're the guy who goes shopping but is too poor to buy anything but bones. Bones, bones, bones, every week. No offence meant to good old Chenjerai Hove, of course. A girl you've been telling grand tales about yourself sees you collecting your miserable parcel and what do you say to her in self-defence? "Er, hi, Gaudencia. What on earth are you doing, er, here? My dog has such an appetite you wouldn't, er, believe how many bones it eats every day, er, Gau!" See, Piri. You can't beat me at this.'

'What about this one? A gardener called Brown suspects his wife of having an affair with a man called Giant, whom he has never seen. On a tip from his neighbour Brown arms himself with an axe and goes to confront Giant over the matter. When he knocks on the latter's door, out comes a huge man. Thrown off guard, what does Brown say? "Sorry, sir. Scuse me, sir. *Ndiri kutengesa matemo*. I'm selling axes. Would you like to buy this sharp one, sir?"'

'We've heard that one before. Haven't we, Mai George?'

'Okay, Loveness, here's a new one. Surely you'll love this. You know Privilege is a man with a little education and a modest job. He's happily married with two young children, but for eight months of the year his wife is in the rural areas, tending their little farm. Privilege of course visits her as often as he can. When his wife falls pregnant for the third time, he's thrilled. He tells his colleagues at work, "I'm going to see the children." But we all know who he's really going to "see"! Now from his rusty biology and his good SaManyika instincts, Privilege is convinced the baby grows in segments, and that with each essential coupling the baby acquires a vital new part. One weekend his bus leaves without him. Running after it, he yells "Stop, stop, driver! My baby still needs a thorax!"'

'Shame. Shame.'

'Shame. Shame. Now stop sounding like those good, little, old white "Medems".'

'Poor Piri.'

'Try again!'

'You're getting old and rueful, Biscuit. Look at your head, white as asbestos dust. Old as … who was it in the Bible? Methuselah? Are you working in a maize mill? Now that Kumbudzi Cemetery is full, have you booked yourself a grave at Greendale? Dying is getting more expensive, you know. By the shovelful. Your ghost will be pretty lonely if you choose to be buried in the deserted rural areas, or, worse still, on the new farms. Perhaps we ought to start local ghost clubs.'

'Cremation might not be a bad idea, after all ...'

'Just be sure not to snort up your father's ashes with your snuff or whatever, like that Rolling Stone fellow, what's-his-name?'

'Keith Richards.'

'Hey, guys, did you read about the Grade 7 boy who raped his own grandmother?'

'Yuk! He should be castrated at once.'

'Exit Operation Murambatsvina. Enter Operation Castration.'

'There's a new job for you, Goriati. You are manly enough. Cadet Officer, Castration Unit. Previous experience with animals a decided advantage. At least one A-level pass required. Bring your own pliers.'

'No thank you. I'm a book-keeper, man.'

'Did you hear about your cousin the economist who, on being pressed by his old grandmother to describe the nature of his work, lamely replied, '*Ah, Mbuya, basa rangu nderokunyima mari* – my job is to be stingy with money.'

'And the guy who married his own mother?'

'No need to blunt your pliers with this one, Goriati. Good luck to him with his mother-in-law, whoever and wherever she is.'

'And if they have children together how would the children address them?'

'God knows.'

'Laugh, Mai George, laugh. *Itai chikwee chaicho!* You never laugh. It's good for you, you know. It's good for your thorax. It eases the muscles of your mandibles. It tickles your little hooves. You are not the one who betrayed Jesus, you know. You didn't sign the country away with an 'X' tremulously inked in at the bottom of a piece of paper with ant-like print. You didn't invade any farm. You didn't send your husband away or starve your children. You didn't run away with the man next door ...'

'And the man or woman next door is always sweet as a cold quart of Castle Lager, Spoo.'

'You mean a good, cold beer is as sweet as somebody else's husband or wife.'

'Hear, hear.'

'Laugh, sister. We can't all be chefs, you know. We're hwakaz.'

'Hwakaz of the world unite!'

'Yeah.'

'Maybe Mai George laughs in her dreams. Maybe she even dreams in full colour.'

'Leave her alone. She works very hard. She's tired.'

'If you need a new husband tell me and I'll fetch you one any time, Mai George.'

'There you go, Fambi. Waiting to pounce on innocent women with your rotten claws. Who told you every woman needs a husband?'

'Sorry, Pretty. Just jokes. But if I tried you would you say yes, Pretty?'

'Not if you were the last man left in the Mash West Province.'

'Nonsense. I already finished with you in my dreams.'

'How about this one, guys?'

'Oh, shut up, Million!'

'During one of the most prolonged ZESA load-shedding exercises a woman returned from a trip to the rural areas to find her children huddled in the dark house. "Oh my poor babies," she said with concern. "Weren't you afraid of the dark while I was away?"

'"No," replied the youngest child, innocently. "We weren't afraid. But I think *baba* was scared stiff because most nights he moved in with *sisi* in the spare bedroom."'

'You haven't heard this one. A prostitute says to a prospective client, "All right, Uncle. I usually work on commission. You say you're not rich. I'll make it easy for you. I'll give you a discount. Why don't you start me off with the equivalent of a teacher's monthly salary for tonight? Half of that for short time."'

'Teachers, nurses …'

'Soldiers, too.'

'Oh, please. Give them a break.'

'And, Mai George, surely you'll like this one. A ranting, raving, Bible-thumping pastor who had made a second vocation out of stalking other men's wives had his congregation in stitches when he plucked a woman's bright red knickers out of his suit pocket and wiped his forehead with them, thinking it was his handkerchief ... and announced, "I haven't finished yet ..." Eh, Mai George?'

***

She had finished sweeping and tidying up her room and was dusting the headboard on which lay the photo albums of her husband and children, bound copies of her CV and job application letters, when she heard the familiar knock, rather, an insistent bang, on her door. She turned down the TV.

'Mai George! Mai George! Open up!'

She undid the bolts and threw open the door of the cottage and in stepped Mbuya MaSibanda, her landlady. The lady wore a crimson nightgown that breathed a cheap perfume and parted in the middle to expose a black petticoat silhouetting a bony frame that had seen many nights. Her hair was coiled ominously on top of her head and her cheeks were smothered with rouge. Since she'd moved in two months ago, Mai George had never seen her outside of that gown or with her hair down.

Mbuya MaSibanda planted herself on the immaculate double bed and surveyed the neatly wallpapered room and the children's clothes, still new in their plastic wraps. 'My, my, do we have a colour TV now!'

'Yes, Mbuya,' Mai George responded, awkwardly.

'Double bed, wardrobe, fridge, hot-plate and TV. Aren't we doing well!'

'Thank you, Mbuya.'

'There's just one slight problem with the TV, *mwanangu*. Colour. It attracts thieves, you know. And with Murambatsvina, every other man in the street is now a thief. Even the good Lord, pardon me, Jesus, would become a thief in this country. You know I have a small black and white set in the main house and all the other lodgers haven't got sets. Why didn't you tell me that you were going to buy a colour set?'

'I'm sorry, Mbuya.'

'Well, next time you buy something, let me know. Procedure, you see. That's how I run this place, how I've run this house since my

147

husband died ten years ago, and the good Lord knows Tom Shine was a righteous man, rest his soul, though he smacked me in the face once for fawning over a stranger. And I notice you put a lock block on your door. Why would you do that with me here all day? I mean, should anything happen while you are away – say a fire or a theft – I would need access to your room. Now, *mwanangu*, aren't you going to give me a little bite to eat?'

'I eat at work and hardly bring any food at home, Mbuya.'

'Nothing at all? Not even bare bones from the bottom of your pots? From now on, bring me something to eat in the evenings. A little dish for your old landlady? I've heard about your excellent cooking, and your customers. How about a warm cup of tea and some biscuits then?'

While Mai George was switching on the kettle, Mbuya MaSibanda examined the photo album.

'This your husband and these your little babies?'

'Yes, Mbuya.'

'And you said he's been gone three years?'

'Yes, Mbuya.'

'Botswana, eh?'

'And does he send you pulas?'

'Sometimes,' she lied.

'I'll talk to you if I ever need pulas. Don't worry. He might come back or he might not. Men are funny creatures. Lecherous as goats, most of them. Just keep working for your children. Don't throw yourselves at the wolves. You said you want to go to secretarial college, don't you? Good idea. Take a leaf from my book. I've lived clean and alone for ten years, but you'll notice people gossip about me left, right and centre because my house and cottage were built with an approved plan. They know, and are jealous, that Murambatsvina can't touch me. Any men you see coming here are my children or relatives seeking help and very few of them ever put up in the house.'

Mai George poured her the tea, and as Mbuya MaSibanda munched a biscuit and took a sip, her lipstick melted into a red wound that stained the yellow mug.

'Just a few more little things, Mai George. Please don't leave your windows wide open at weekends because it finishes fresh air for the other lodgers. Disturbs the circulation, you see. And don't watch your new TV too long. It's bad for your eyes and colour TV chews up more electricity than black and white.'

Mbuya MaSibanda balanced her cup carefully in the saucer and went on, hardly drawing breath, 'Also, you haven't been taking a turn to sweep the yard and scrub the toilet in the morning as all my lodgers should.'

'But I asked Mai Tariro next door to do my turn for me, Mbuya MaSibanda. I even pay her to do it.'

'You pay her. That's a bad precedent, *mwanangu*. It might breed the dangerous misconception that, because of money, some lodgers are free from duties and more important than others.'

'But I have to leave home at four in the morning, Mbuya MaSibanda, and you want the sweeping and scrubbing done at seven.'

'In which case you might have to leave for work after seven when it's your turn.'

Mai George stared at her TV and, as the meaning of the remark dawned on her, she snorted with half reckless abandon, 'Maybe I'd need to look for another room elsewhere.'

'Oh, you would,' Mbuya MaSibanda retorted, her eyes suddenly flickering with fire. 'You would, then? Good luck with Murambatsvina. In any case I was going to treble your rent next month. The dollar is going down and your business is booming and there are dozens of people asking for your room every week. See, child, that's the name of the game.'

'And will you get anybody to pay you that much? Will you? Or you will put in one of your "husbands"?'

Mai George glared at the older woman sitting on her bed sipping her tea. Mbuya MaSibanda seemed to age years in those seconds. Suddenly her soap and perfume took on a rank odour, like cat's urine, and her eyes blinked ashes. Her lips and hands shook and her fingers wrinkled with hate. Mai George felt like snatching the mug from her and smashing it into her teeth and only just stopped herself from doing so. Then something happened to Mai George, something that she had kept locked up for a long time escaped, her sense of the absurd. She straightened up, caught herself from drowning in the rubble of her former self. A rush of air cleared her chest and her lungs heaved. She felt her cheeks twitch and the first cackle tweaked the insides of her ribs; a mere titter, a snicker, a chuckle, a chortle, swelled into a gurgle. Her sides shook uncontrollably; she giggled; then heard herself slowly explode into a guffaw. The force of her roar banged the asbestos roofing of the cottage, rattled the plates off the shelf, thrummed the rats out of the cracked walls, scuttled the spiders out of the broken floor, whooshed her papers onto the bed, tossed the mug of hot tea out of the old lady's trembling hand and hurried her out. Bravely following Mbuya MaSibanda to the door and shooing her out, almost, Mai George began to LAUGH. She laughed freely now. She laughed and laughed; she laughed at the brazen jokes that had plagued her day, at the sudden future that now glared in her face. She laughed and heard the voices of the other lodgers in the adjoining rooms shrieking with hers, conspiring with her against the ageless tyranny of the world. Her ears drowned in the echoes of her mirth as warm tears coursed down her youthful face.

Infidel

1

Huge white tent at the edge of the township's grey houses. Every evening that week. Stark against the curly blue smoke of little chimneys and the dull glitter of tins and broken bottles in the rubbish dumps. Singing, testifying and praying all night. Grade 6 boy. Eleven, twelve, bald head. Long-legged. Knock-kneed. Buck teeth. Round, bright hungry eyes. Ears fleeing from knife-thin face. Huge tent. Large open truck in tent. Microphones, speakers, stereos. Black and white preachers. Little blue and green cars for white Messiahs parked in the road, at the edge of the black township. Young white priest. 'Who wants to accept Jesus into his heart tonight? Who wants to be saved by the Lord? Come out to the front and accept the Lord tonight. Come out and be redeemed by the blood of the lamb. Come out and be *saaaaved!*' Voice like a magnet. Commanding, 'Come out to the front all ye lost sheep! Rise up and come!' He, the Grade 6 boy. Seized by the ferment. Squirming in the white plastic chair. Rising slowly. Stepping out towards that voice. Drawn by its soft magnetic power. 'Yes, I see that, Sir. Yes, I see that, Ma'am. Yes, I see that child.' Grade 6 boy. Rising and fumbling through the crowd to the front. 'Come, child.' The front. Figures kneeling in the open. On the grass. Stepping out to the front on watery feet. Shaky soles. Heart pounding. Mind in turmoil. Figures gathering in the open space at the front. Kneel. Down onto knees. On the grass. Chips of stone biting into bare flesh. Eyes half closed. Head gripped by firm white hand. Mouth quivering. Ears roaring. 'Yes,

151

child. Open up, child. Welcome, child.'

***

In the new, cacophonous family of the saved, a young white woman gave him a little bound copy of the New Testament, a sugary doughnut and a cream soda. Fleshy hands shook his small one with firm grips. Strong soft chests hugged against his. Faces beamed at him. A smile twitched at his lips. His mouth opened to sing.

***

He went home to another meatless supper. Cold, howling night. Banana trees shivering, as always, in the half dark. Paint peeling from summer-sodden walls. Low, scowling asbestos roof. His heart warm like a secret brazier. His soul glowing brighter than candlelight. Cosier than smoke.

His mother blew blindly at the thick lichened wood in the stove and said, 'Where were you again?'

Every evening that week, he went to the tent. At school, newly saved, he avoided rubbing shoulders with the unsavoury herd of the unsaved, the sinners. He kept his head low, picked his words carefully, spoke in a hush of liquid phrases. He smiled at everyone who came his way, dispensed with swearing and bad words, performed constant little acts of goodness so that his guardian angel could tick him off on the daily score-board of his new life. He moved on undaunted even when after giving a beggar ten cents, the tattered man threw it back at him and spitting, 'Take back your dirty money! Son of a whore!' He prayed. He prayed every morning and every night, singing new songs inside his chest, '*I will make you fishers of men...*' Yes, he'd been fished from sin but at home there wasn't a single fish in a fortnight for him or his small siblings. He looked up hungrily at the moon where Neil Armstrong and his mates had stepped out into the dead dust one cold morning. God must have been looking out for the astronauts and their spacecraft so that they would not get too close to the roof of heaven. But where was heaven? Did the other planets in the solar system have the same God and the same heaven too? Were there people out there? And angels, too? Did the angels wear space suits? But there was no spacecraft mentioned in the Bible. Perhaps it was there, buried somewhere in the Book of Revelations. He said to his grandmother, grandmother cleaning, with a crooked, wizened finger, her mean plate of *rupiza* – lentil porridge – the old woman squatting on the polished, cracked floor like a spotted brown bullfrog, choking with mysterious rage and discomfort, 'Mbuya, Mbuya, did you know a man stepped onto the moon, that full round moon up there in the sky, last night?' Mbuya growled back, 'What nonsense is this now? *Tibvire pano, iwe kapenzi!* Off with you, miscreant!' She smelled very bad. She had just come from her village somewhere. She did not like taking a bath. The smell of her filled the house. She reeked of the time trapped in the crevices of her ageless skirts. Mother put a large zinc *bhavhu* of hot water in the 'shower' and said to her, 'Time for your bath, Gogo.' When she was cleansed she stretched out on the floor in the kitchen; fed pinches of snuff to her nostrils and hummed ominous old tunes to herself. He half wished she could go back to the village she had come from but now, because he had accepted the Lord in his breast, he quickly banished the selfish thoughts from his head.

***

At his *real* church, the preacher droned on in a low voice; it was not like the tent. Here, at his *real* church, you were baptised as an infant, then Sunday-schooled, then catechised and 'confirmed' so that you could eat and drink *chirairo*, the Holy Communion, with the elders. You did not rise up in church and shout, 'Amen!' back at the preacher! You did not dance with joy. You did not shake or foam at the mouth or fall at the pulpit. It wasn't like at the tent. Here adults spent weeks praying and repenting, preparing, laundering their souls up for *chirairo*. Adults seemed to worship just so that they could eat and drink the next *chirairo*. If you were *pasi peshamhu yekereke*, under the church's cane of chastisement, like VaDhewa's daughter Spiwe who had fallen pregnant in Form 2, you did not eat *chirairo* for a specified period.

One Sunday afternoon he ran up to his mother and panted, 'Mother, mother, did the *chirairo* taste good today?' She smacked him on the cheek and elbowed him out of the way. For a person who had just partaken of the communion, she was a bit too hard on him, he thought.

Once a year, in the townships, all the members of the real churches (which had solid brick walls, windows, roofs and hard wooden benches – not tents), gathered together for a combined service. On the 'big' Sunday of that season, all the men, women and children assembled in the large Methodist Hall and Mfundisi Manda preached his dramatic sermon in Chichewa. VaDhewa, whose daughter Spiwe was under the cane of chastisement for falling pregnant in Form 2, translated into Shona. But the sermon was so exciting that when Mufundisi Manda said 'Murungu', meaning God, VaDhewa kept repeating the word as if it meant 'white person' and not God. Nobody minded. Everyone nodded or grunted righteously and urged him on. But people said VaDhewa stocked up food in the wardrobe in the bedroom and rationed it to his wife, whom he beat up every so often for one transgression or another.

One Sunday at their own church when Reverend Mabwe was away and Baba Mebo had been 'given the plan' for the day, the latter preached a sermon about a man who could speak many languages and was often called upon to translate sermons at combined church services, but he also rationed food to his wife and regularly beat her up. Halfway through the scathing parable, VaDhewa called out from the audience, with ominous calm, 'Preach the gospel, Baba Mebo, don't preach about an individual!' Baba Mebo stopped, mid-sentence, closed his Bible and sat down. Suddenly everyone was shaking their heads and whispering urgently and VaDhewa was banging on the pulpit and yelling, 'I can kill, me! I've spilt blood, me. You all, you don't know me!' The service broke up in confusion and after that Baba Mebo became strangely quiet.

In Grade 7, aged twelve, he passed his *katikazi*, his catechism. The catechist, VaMhungu, who loaded and hauled bags of roller meal over his hefty shoulders all day at Rhodesia Milling, donned his unmistakable coffee-coloured suit and thin grey tie on Sundays, and insisted that answers be correct to the very last syllable – as proclaimed in the catechist's handbook. So it was that at last he ate and drank *chirairo* with the elders, tasting, for the first time, the dry, brittle bread melting on the tip of his tongue and the sweet, giddy warmth of the red wine in his throat – Christ's flesh and blood. He had imagined *chirairo* to be some feast substantial enough to satisfy the earthly appetite and was surprised at the diminutive flakes. But then, he reasoned, the body of Christ had to be served thriftily to feed every mouth everywhere in the world and at so many communions.

But with the memory of the firm grip of that white, Pentecostal hand in the huge white tent still lingering in his head and his heart, as well as his recent confirmation, which gave him the right to partake of *chirairo* at his own church, he felt doubly saved, even purer to face the world.

2

In Form 1, at the Government boarding school, he happily enlisted in the Scripture Union. He was issued with a leather-bound Gideon's Bible, a song and prayer book and a badge. The members sang, testified and prayed every Sunday, for the poor, the sick and those languishing in prison. He donated, from the two dollars his father doled out to him every term as pocket money, little alms for the destitute, squeezing precious money-box pennies into the kitty of his bourgeoning faith.

Sometimes the Scripture Union organised excursions to neighbouring farms or camping spots where they would meet and hold hands with white people and 'coloureds', students, teachers, pastors brought together by The Spirit and he would be swept up in the big, bounteous, harmonious wave of those multicoloured, mixed race, mixed age gatherings. He felt oneness with The Lord as the Being he could chat to, any and every hour. He had no other care in the world but this, for His Saviour, and except perhaps also for his meals and studies.

He kept himself scrupulously clean in thought and deed, diligently avoiding smoking, drinking, pilfering, petty bullying, truancy, midnight mealie-raiding forays to the farms and various acts of abuse, self-inflicted and otherwise, which were rife in the dorms. He shunned the Sunday afternoon 'see me' sessions where he feared he could be trapped by some sly member of the opposite sex. He read his Bible, prayed every night and stuck to his books.

One day Alice, the belle of the class, who already happened to possess a slightly protuberant bust, rocked her chest at him and wiggled her small, wet, pink tongue to his face. Trembling with shock and disgust, he hissed, 'Get thee behind me, Alice. My father sacrificed everything to send me here to get a decent education and I have no time to waste. Besides, the Good Lord would not approve...'

There followed much jeering laughter and amusement in the classroom and, deeply hurt, he fled into the corridor.

***

Billet Ngara was the treasurer of the Scripture Union. He was in the upper sixth, and studying English, history, divinity and the general paper and he was oh, so divine in his crisp white shirt and smart grey longs. (The younger boys wore khaki shirts and shorts.) Billet smiled vaingloriously and explained to him that, in the sixth form, what was called Bible knowledge at O-level broadened into a new discipline called 'divinity', which included studies of other world religions and beliefs. Billet was also on the 'editorial board' (he looked the phrase up) of the school magazine. The eager young first-former showed him his prospective entry for the publication, a rhyming, six-stanza poem titled 'School children'. The poem ran:

> Good school children everywhere
> Are always very rare
> You just can't find the sort of things
> To please these ailing beings
> Ask the children of this school
> What they hate and like to do
> And you almost can be sure
> They'll never tell what's true
> Sports and games, they do like them
> 'Coz the school earns a bit of fame'
> Punishment is quite a bad song
> Although they know they're wrong...

'Beautiful, Godfrey,' Billet stroked the soft down on his chin, 'Beautiful. I'll definitely have it published in the magazine.'

Godfrey asked if 'published' meant the same as 'printed' and Billet smiled and nodded.

The sixth-former became his surrogate brother and friend. He read Godfrey's compositions and poems and showed them to his

156

classmates and said, 'We'll make an author of you yet, Godi.' Billet smiled his slow white smile and explained that 'author' was really just a bigger word for 'writer'. Often he would call him to his locker in the sixth form dorm and give him biscuits, cool drinks or bread with slices of corned beef. Godfrey toyed with and then quickly stamped out the suspicion that perhaps his older friend could afford generous supplies of tuck because of his position in the union. He, in turn, asked to read Billet's general-paper essays, one of which was '"Religion is the opium of the masses": Karl Marx. Discuss.' Godfrey read the essay repeatedly, eventually asking Billet, 'Who's Karl Marx? What's opium? What is meant by the "masses"?' Billet said he need not worry about such terms in Form 1; and that he would explain them later.

One day Billet said, 'I want to do something very special for you this week, Godfrey.'

'What something, *mkoma*?'

'Something *very, very* special.'

'Can you tell me, *mkoma*?'

'You needn't know now.'

'Can't you give me a little hint?'

'It's something very, very special for you. Let's keep it a secret between you and me. You'll know soon enough.' They went together to the evening prayers.

That week was 'Week of Witness' for the Scripture Union. The union members called it 'WOW!' They sang and prayed every night. Godfrey wondered what surprise Mkoma Billet wanted to spring on him. Billet was the treasurer and a powerful member of the Scripture Union. Perhaps he had arranged for him to go on a trip outside the country! Or even secured a bursary for him. And, of course, he could have found a willing publisher (or, was it a printer?) for his 'Poems and General Works, 1971', which he had often promised he would try to do! And he might have bought him presents, most likely books, stationery or clothes, a designer T-shirt or pair of socks; a tennis racket would do nicely, thank you. Not to rule out a possible holiday attachment, open to young, persevering members of the SU, at the organisation's headquarters in the city ...

He fantasised and fantasised about the possibilities.

The week dragged by. Billet kept mum about the nature of his promise. Godfrey grew tense with anticipation. That Saturday evening Billet took him to the little SU office behind the Beit Hall. There was a full moon and the night was warm and dripping with the sap of the pine trees growing outside the hall. A bat swooped over them. Billet inserted a long key into the door and turned it. The door opened into the tiny room. He switched on the light and drew up a small, hard chair. The walls of the room were lined with books. Godfrey had never been there before. Billet sat down opposite him.

'Well, Godfrey,' he beamed. 'Here's your surprise! What did you think I would do for you, eh?'

Godfrey blinked under the harsh light of the single naked bulb dangling from the ceiling.

'I'll give you a little hint. This is WOW! Week of Witness. I bring you a special present, Godfrey. What did you think I would do for you, Godfrey? Confess.'

There was no parcel in the room. Billet had brought no envelopes with him, no tell-tale papers and there was no promising bulge in his pockets. Billet cackled softly. Godfrey squinted and grinned weakly at him.

'I bring you not worldly gifts but salvation for your soul, Godfrey,' he coughed importantly. 'Are you saved, Godfrey?'

Godfrey nodded blankly.

'I mean really *saved*, Godfrey?'

'I was baptised as a child.'

'I know you may have been baptised, or confirmed; you may even have taken communion,' Billet cut him off.

'Once, when I was in Grade 6…'

'Yes, once what?'

He wanted to tell Billet about the evening in the big white tent, but words failed him; his lips twitched wordlessly. He'd never confessed that incident to anyone and the memory of it pricked like a penknife. His eyes strayed over the narrow, cracked wooden table.

Billet licked his lips with a flourish.

'It is not enough to sing and pray in the Scripture Union, or any church for that matter. The SU is merely a vehicle for your deliverance. Today you will accept Jesus personally into your heart and you will be *saved* once and for all. I'll guide you through that. God has chosen you and sent me to deliver his message. That is the special present I bring you during this WOW! Here, put your hands in mine and repeat after me.'

Billet clasped Godfey's hands and prayed. He prayed loud and long; the small boy's voice voice trailed feebly after his loud one.

'Open your heart and accept Jesus, Godfrey. I command you to do so now. You will do as I say. Do you accept Him as your Saviour? Think of heaven and everlasting bliss; hell and eternal fire. I bring you a passport to heaven, my dear brother.'

Godfrey opened his eyes and saw Billet's tightly bunched eyelids, his anxious, moist lips and the soft down on his chin. He felt the grip of his soft hands; that half familiar grip claiming his soul again.

'Open up your heart this minute, Godfrey. Do you accept him, yes or no?'

'I accept him.'

'Louder!'

'I ACCEPT HIM.'

'With all your heart?'

'With all my heart.'

'Splendid, splendid,' Billet gave his hands a sudden relieved squeeze and breathed in like a prize-winning swimmer emerging from the water for a final triumphal gulp of air. 'Let's pray again.'

Later that night, after they had knelt and sung several hymns, as he was led out of the stark light of that small room into the soft moonlight of the courtyard, Godfrey thought he felt a bat skimming ominously over them both as his head bumped against a tree trunk. Laughing gently, Billet took his hand in his, but he jerked free.

Stumbling blindly after Billet, back to the raucous dorms, he felt a strange slow anger swelling in his chest.

***

When he was a first year undergraduate at the university and Godfrey

159

was in Form 2, Billet happened to be passing through his young friend's hometown and arranged to visit him. In great excitement, Godfrey weeded and watered the flower beds, the path and the small vegetable garden patch, helped his mother polish the floors, dust the furniture and clean the windows of their small, four-roomed township house. Sure enough, Mkoma Billet turned up, strolling down the street with one hand folded familiarly against his breast. Godfrey ran to meet him.

His mother fussed over their important guest. She made eggs, sausages, bread and coffee for him (she had sent Godfrey to buy a small packet of the beverage, normally they had tea). His father asked important questions about university and the Scripture Union, clearly overwhelmed that their young son had been singled out by this exemplary student as his surrogate brother and friend, and stressing that he wanted Godfrey to emulate the young man. As usual, Godfrey's father was eager to show that he had a few things to say to the youth of the day about life in general. Billet sat half sunken in the sagging sofa, eating, listening, talking and laughing affably as if he had been to the house and met with them a dozen times before – young Godfrey had every reason to be proud to be associated with him.

'Wonderful friend you have,' his father congratulated him after Billet had left.

***

The two friends wrote regularly to each other. On Billet's invitation, Godfrey visited him in his room at the university. He showed him the campus and together they had lunch in the dining room – mushroom soup, huge T-bone steaks, mashed potatoes and green peas, and then vanilla ice-cream, an unusual treat after his accustomed boarding-school fare. Billet introduced him to his friends of all colours, many of whom belonged to the university branch of the Scripture Union. Everyone was amused at how young, serious and ambitious he was, to visit the campus at fifteen when he was only in Form 3! On being introduced to the branch chairman, a lean white fellow with a hollowed stomach, red eyes and sagging jeans, Godfrey said, 'Pleased to meet you, Sir,' to which the other laughed and replied, 'The name's Tom and I'm just a bum, mate.'

'What do you want to become when you get older?' Tom asked him.

'An author,' he replied, primly.

'What do you plan to study at university?'

'Authorship.'

'But they don't teach authorship at university. To be an author you need to live life in order to write about it. You'll probably have to study the arts and become a chalk-and-talk master like the rest of us, while you accumulate experience.'

'What's a chalk-and-talk master?'

'Can't you guess? You seem like a bright young fellow.'

'He means a teacher,' Billet explained.

'That, or a journalist perhaps, but you know things are not very nice in the country and good old Smithy isn't very kind to black journalists and their ilk. You might end up languishing in prison, ha, ha!'

Billet was reading English and divinity, studying to become a high-school teacher. He invited Godfrey to help him with an assignment – calling it 'Prac. Crit.' – on an untitled poem, which he subsequently discovered was 'Pianos and Drums' by the West African poet, Gabriel Okara. Billet let Godfrey read the poem several times before asking him what he thought it meant. Godfrey intuited that there were two ways of life described in the poem, one to do with pianos, and the other with drums. Pianos stood for the modern way of doing things, and drums for the old. He fumbled for words to express the point. Billet reclaimed the poem from him and explained.

'Can't you see, Godfrey? Pianos stand for Christian salvation and drums represent hell and damnation. The two can never work together. You have to make a choice.'

'Why can't they work together?' Godfrey ventured.

'Can you be saved and still go to the countryside to play drums to evil traditional spirits, for instance?'

'Some people do.'

'But do *you*? Does *your* family? You were saved at last year's Week of Witness. Your parents, though they may not have received *direct* salvation in their church, are dedicated worshippers. You wouldn't go to such ceremonies, would you?'

'Some of our relatives do. My father's brother, for instance.'

'Then they're all damned! *Damned!* You hear?'

'So are my great, great grandparents damned too?'

'If they were not washed in the blood of Jesus, yes.'

'But what about those who died before the arrival of the missionaries and the Pioneer Column in 1890?'

'They are damned as well.'

'The whole lot of them? All those hundreds of thousands of people who believed in ancestor worship? Is that fair?'

'It's not a question of fairness. Faith comes before fairness. Well, some of them might be judged according to their works. Anyway, you need not worry about them. God will know what to do with them. I'll tell you who you should worry about, and that's *you* and *your* soul.'

'What about those people who might have heard about Jesus but not properly understood about Him and his word?'

'Damned, too!'

'And those who choose simply not to heed Him?'

'Fodder for fire and brimstone.'

'What about those who do not believe in the Bible and belong to other religions, for instance Moslems, Hindus, Buddhists, Sihks, Animists…?'

'Who's been talking to you about this, Godfrey?'

'Nobody.'

'Beware of blasphemy, my friend. Blasphemy is one of the biggest sins. It's almost unforgivable. And when you're judged on judgement day, nobody will be there to help you. Not even your guardian angel. It'll just be you and your Maker.'

The discussion had drifted away from the poem and things were turning ugly. Godfrey had not meant to provoke his host but merely to state that he believed that in the poem, as in life, different beliefs and ways of being could co-exist, even complement each other; but it would be years before he could explain life that way. And, even then, Godfrey was shocked at his own daring.

And here was Billet, Billet with soft down on his chin; Billet, the fisherman, greedy to beach more lost souls and chalk up more points on the score board of his existence; Billet the second-year undergraduate, gathering his papers, clucking his tongue and fuming softly under his breath. 'Anyway, Godfrey, you can't really help me with this. You're too young and green. I only wanted to introduce you to practical criticism and perhaps this poem was not the best choice to begin with. Never mind, I'll write my paper alone later.'

It was nearly time to go. There was a knock on the door and a woman came in. She had a small, hardened body and a shorn head that gave her an indeterminate age. She wore a pink maternity dress and loose-fitting green slippers and was clearly pregnant. Billet cleared the bed of papers so that she could sit down and said, casually, 'Godfrey, this is Pamela, my wife-to-be. Pamela, this is my young friend, Godfrey, whom I've often talked about.'

Pamela shook his hand hesitantly; her own was small and rather hard. She gave him a wistful smile, her dark narrow eyes keenly surveying him.

'Pamela teaches at a primary school in DZ,' Billet said. 'She and I are going to wed soon. You will be duly invited, of course.'

On the way back to school, Godfrey thought about Billet and Pamela. He reasoned that if Pamela was already a trained primary school teacher then she was roughly his friend's age, perhaps even slightly older. And if she was pregnant, she was pregnant out of wedlock. Had the pregnancy been a mistake? Or had she trapped Billet, a prospective university *graduate*, into marriage? God, please no. Were they arranging a hasty marriage in order to legitimise their union and the coming baby? Had they not transgressed the rules of the Bible by having sex before marriage? And how was it that Billet had not told him about his engagement? Would, indeed, he have done so, if Pamela had not walked into the room? Was she a secret about which Billet was ashamed?

***

The wedding was a flop.

Both Billet's and Pamela's families boycotted the service because they had not been properly informed or invited. Protocol had not been observed. In Christian zeal, the two had chosen to defy tradition. No lobola had been paid. There wasn't even a *munyai*, a go-between, sent to propose the union and ease its passage.

The ceremony took place in the cramped hall at the school where Pamela was teaching. Not even the school head attended. A distant cousin gave away the bride, out of a dingy store-room, and a university colleague in the union conducted the short service. There were no bridesmaids, no best men to accompany the couple; the gospel music sputtered out of a scratchy stereo.

The guests were mainly uniformed school children, conscripted from the classrooms, a handful of colleagues from the Scripture Union and Pamela's mainly female fellow teachers. Her belly ballooned through her cheap white wedding dress while Pamela fidgeted on a small, hard, classroom chair, her swollen face visibly sweating, her hands clutching a small bouquet, probably gathered from the school gardens. In a hired, oversized black suit and bow-tie, Billet leant back on his seat, fingers drumming on the low table, clearly wishing the ordeal was over. There was no rice or chicken; the guests had cool drinks and plain buns. A small amount of cash was collected in a metal plate.

Clad in a tight-fitting, striped, grey suit with wide bell-bottoms, Godfrey leant over to chat to the newly-weds.

'You see, Godfrey,' Billet explained, wiping his brow with a khaki handkerchief and straightening his bow-tie, 'Pamela and I decided to make this a really small affair, just to make us man and wife. Nothing grand, you know. Maybe, in the future, when we're settled and the baby's born, we'll organise something grander…'

Godfrey grinned and nodded but he felt washed by a profound sadness.

3

Eight very short years later, Godfrey himself married, in similar circumstances. He was barely one year out of university and not even launched into the joys and rhythms of working life when his girlfriend

Vhaidha, his first-ever, proper 'partner', fell pregnant. They signed their union in church and the wizened priest, at snail pace, fussed over the pen, the nibs and ink and papers. Godfrey's younger brother and Vhaidha's younger sister witnessed and signed the certificates. The church was empty. There was no ceremony and no guests. They were not even dressed for the event: Godfrey wore a black T-shirt and faded jeans, she, a red maternity dress and blue rubber slippers. The priest's voice was muffled in the quiet gloom as he blew on the ink to dry it.

Their fate was sealed. Now the coming baby would be born in wedlock, legitimately set forth into the world. They would bravely have to learn to live together as man and wife. With the precious piece of paper they could get income-tax rebates, better rented accommodation, and various other perks.

But with it went their individual freedoms.

Mkoma Billet did not grace the occasion. He was nowhere to be found. The two friends had slowly lost contact; perhaps the older man had left to pursue further Bible studies in Australia, sponsored by the Scripture Union. Later they would bump into each other in a supermarket, Godfrey pushing a trolley half full of beers, Billet sporting a comfortable potbelly and Pamela buxomly herding a brood of children. Billet said, shaking his head, 'So, you're drinking now, Godfrey?' He told his old friend that he was now a pastor and his wife was studying to be one too.

At first the church-going habit remained with Godfrey; like the proverbial iron shirt, it could not be cast off. He had long weaned himself away from the Scripture Union. He had married Vhaidha because he'd made her pregnant, because her parents belonged to the same church as his parents, because her father was a deacon and because his parents were friends. Frankly, he had done it for them! Godfrey could not shame them all, oh no. And that was the biggest mistake of his life. He loved Vhaidha, or thought he did, but that he'd married so early, at twenty-three, when he was just starting out in life and the world was full of other possibilities, was something that hurt him like a sore rib.

On Sundays he went to the city church with Vhaidha and the baby, even when he had a hangover. But he hated it when the preacher asked him to pray and he stood up, closed his eyes and fumbled with unconvincing clichés, with words and phrases that he no longer, perhaps had never *really*, believed. He hated it even more when, after the service, they had to drop in on Vhaidha's parents, whose house was near the church, where they were asked to stay for tea or for lunch and obliged to engage in protracted small talk.

Meanwhile Vhaidha immersed herself in the life of the church, zestfully attending the married women's club, all-night prayer meetings, funerals, weddings and church bazaars.

Slowly, he grew to hate the church, and because she loved it so much, he began to hate her too. He felt she looked down on him because of his waning faith. He longed to unshackle himself from the church, and from her. The two became inseparable. When she left their old church to join the newest Pentecostal denomination in town he hated her even more.

4

During the 1990s, as the economy went downhill, the new Pentecostal churches invaded the country with a vengeance. When he was a child, he could count off all the big conventional churches on the fingers of his hands, but now the emergent churches had mushroomed throughout the land. They put up tents, bought up shops, hotels, restaurants and bars and converted them into places of worship, purchased open land from the city council and erected factory-size churches. Some of the wealthier ones erected structures the size of airport buildings. The churches had spectacular names like Joy Eternal, Rhythm of the Word, Come Feel the Vibes, The Bible Generation, River of Salvation, One Universe, Fountain of Hope, First Envoy, Lake of Solace, Worldwide Witness, Spring of Deliverance, Mission Resurrection, The Lord's Battalion, Blessings Galore, Certainty of Hope, Heaven's Gate, Ark of Redemption, Righteous Will, Manna for All, Covenant of Truth, Chariot of Remembrance, Haven of Love and Live Action Now! They emblazoned the streets and walls with their posters and banners.

Unlike the traditional churches, very, very few built schools, hospitals or clinics. Most preached that if you were rich you were blessed, and if you were poor you were, inevitably, a sinner.

Religion became a commodity and pastorship a way of life.

These churches were ministered to by young clerics, some local, some foreign, male and female, young and not so young, mostly black, who brandished Bibles and for hours on end chanted, bellowed, moaned, groaned, spat and hissed through mountainous PA systems. Many of these pastors were fresh out of Bible college, others received on-the-spot training in improvised crash courses, or simply woke up hearing the word of God. A good number of the novice priests were in their mid-twenties and early thirties and wore exhausted shirts with frayed, stiffly optmistic collars; some were not yet married or propertied and still slept on the floor in single-room quarters, biding their time. They were not discouraged. They took it upon themselves to counsel their eager and often older congregants on love, marriage, family, sickness, adversity, divorce, bereavement, salvation and other weighty matters of life and death which they had themselves scarcely begun to experience.

Those who ran the more established congregations drove Mercedes Benzes, Pajeros and brand new 4x4 twin-cabs and thrived in suburban mansions – their faces glowed with health and good living, as they preached the Gospel of Wealth.

These new pastors recruited ruthlessly from all walks of life. In the past, Bible schools had enlisted teachers approaching middle age, worn down by life and service. Now religion became an open profession, not a vocation. Their target was the huge beleaguered populace suffering from the effects of the economic meltdown, protracted political uncertainty, general moral decay and a complete loss of hope. Once upon a time, Zimbabweans had smugly scoffed at other independent countries 'to the north' which had pandered to the wave of new churches, but now it was we who were swallowing the promised bait, hook, line and sinker.

Song, prayer, testifying and Bible study are now the order of the day. Tithing became another cardinal rule. Joining up is like mortgaging your soul to the big bank of life and forever paying off a fraction of your monthly income to secure your future bliss. Giving to the Lord is a way of asking for blessings, and an investment. The more you give to the church, the more you receive in return. Like cleanliness, material prosperity now sits next to Godliness. Where the rich young man in Matthew 19 was told he must give up everything in order to enter heaven, God, it is now preached, despises poverty – the poor must be sinners – and tacitly approves of the amassing of wealth. To be rich is to be blessed. The latest clothing styles are in vogue. The churches are run like businesses, but no tax is paid to the state. Most of these entities lavish praise on the country's oppressors in order to court favour and avoid official scrutiny. The pastor has become the chief executive of the new 'bank' and he or she can readily cook the books. Few ask how the money is spent; those who are too curious, too close or know too much, can always be paid off.

The pastors of these thriving churches became rich overnight. They have bought themselves mansions and the newest cars, invested in farms and businesses, and sent their children to expensive schools and colleges, often overseas.

And with the acquisition of money came a host of attendant evils.

One male pastor ensnared a chain of willing housewives and took them one by one to bed.

Another, believed to have healing powers, pursued gullible young virgins, extracting sex from them in return for material presents. When they fell pregnant he arranged for them to have abortions and had them implanted with five-year anti-pregnancy devices. A white female pastor flagrantly addicted to stalking young male worshippers of all races stunned everyone when she confessed in front of the congregation that her ten-year-old child was not her husband's, but had been fathered by a married 'boyfriend' who belonged to the same church, and though the husband wept profusely and theatrically announced his immediate forgiveness of his wife (if Jesus could forgive half the world, then why couldn't he, a mere mortal, do so too), the church lost a sizeable number of members who defected back to their original, conventional denominations.

A church with international branches was reputed to be a disguised venue for Satanist practices. Another was openly raising funds by allowing secular events like fashion and musical shows, gambling and political rallies to be held on its premises.

In the fields and open vleis the more traditional and less well-to-do white-garmented flocks swelled in number. They gather at foot-worn spots under the trees, on Wednesdays and Fridays, and at weekends, in rain or cold, day or night. They paint apocalyptic messages on balancing granite rocks by the highways. Many of them refuse to have their children immunised or enrolled in school and despite protracted warnings of AIDS, the elders insist that polygamy is their biblical right. When cholera came it raged through their flocks. They dabbled in a confusing mix of spiritual healing, magic, herbs and sorcery – one of their chief healers was imprisoned for forty years for forcing himself upon ailing women entrusted to his care.

A foreign-based pastor was exposed when the band of the 'sick' and the 'handicapped' whom he so often 'miraculously' healed on the spot at his services turned out to be his disguised accomplices when they reported him to the police with charges of reneging on promised payments.

'I promise you your husband will return to you next week,' another pastor methodically assured the desperate women who pledged up to $500 dollars to his church. And it is said one such returning husband died within a week of rejoining his estranged wife.

'Show them your diamond ring,' yet another pastor urged his wife in the middle of a familiar sermon. 'Tell them we're moving to Borrowdale next month and that they need not remain gardeners and housemaids living in one-roomed lodges all their lives. Tell them no one need ever walk around with less than $200 in their pockets, as long as they pay their tithes. Give them a ride in our new twin cab.'

Unfortunately, the new vehicle got stolen two Sundays later.

Yes, a certain craze hit the land, and it is still with us.

***

So it was that Vhaidha joined one of the newest, wealthiest churches, the Covenant of Truth. The elders of her former church asked her to leave without fanfare to deter other congregants from following suit as they foresaw a looming exodus. She'd already been preaching sermons and leading in women's events in the church of her childhood. Her reason for joining the Covenant, she explained to everyone who questioned her sudden change of allegiance, was that it afforded her 'direct spiritual contact' with God, and a one-to-one relationship with Him.

Her life changed. His life changed. Vhaida went to prayer meetings two or three times a week, and attended two consecutive church services on Sunday. She frequented weddings, funerals, all-night prayer meetings, tithed heavily, and ran a parallel budget to support her new cause. Her wardrobe improved. She bought new outfits and shoes, spruced up her face, her hair and nails. One Sunday when her car was at the garage, and Godfrey went to pick her up in his, she came out to introduce him to her colleagues in the flower-lined car park. In their meticulous clothes, and splendid hair-dos, clasping their fat, leather-bound Bibles in their hands at the end of their creamed arms and deodorized armpits, they looked him up and down, sniffing with their prim noses at his scrappy jeans, worn T-shirt and *manyatera, maJesus* sandals. They turned their faces aside with pity or contempt and he feared they could detect the whiff of last night's booze sweating from his skin.

At home the meals suffered, with the sudden budget cut. Gone went the eggs, sausage and liver in the morning, the accustomed Sunday afternoon steak and mashed potatoes, the spaghetti bolognaise with strawberry and cream desserts on Thursday nights. He would come home and knock on the maid's bedroom and she would wake up and open the door a polite crack and say, adjusting the shoulder of her pink nightdress, with a knowing, little smile, 'Mhamha has gone to an all-night prayer meeting'. Then he would finger the little food left for him, cold sadza, beef shreds and covo – the microwave and the stove had, despite her general prayers, decided to break down again. Sometimes, with a mixture of anger and self-justified relief, he would go back out into the night, returning at dawn, half-gratified but even angrier, spoiling for a fight. She was now demanding money for groceries and the children's uniforms from him, responsibilities that had once been hers.

One day she invited her friends home for a prayer meeting. He was

170

about to make a quick getaway when they started arriving in their cars, blocking his exit. Together, they urged him to join them. There were seven women in their thirties and one small tie-less man in an oversized, striped suit and tiny beige shoes, who had perhaps failed, too late, to evade their net. The women examined the cups and plaques ranged on the mantelpiece and cooed, while he tried to engage the man in small talk.

'You must be making a fortune from all these books, Mr Zimuto,' they murmured with misguided, undisguised envy.

Vhaidha led the Bible Study. She was clearly their leader and kept strictly to matters of faith and supplication. Though she quoted extensively from other books and verses with a conviction and an ease that astounded him, there was nothing personal to her testimony, nothing about her own life. She was another person to *him* then, speaking to *them* like that. Perhaps none of her colleagues even knew about the strife raging within her own household. Secrecy was her lethal weapon.

The youngest and sweetest of the women – her husband had died in a car crash, he later learnt – asked him what his biggest wish was so that they could pray for him. He hesitated and said, 'To be fulfilled,' and she stared at him with her large, thoughtful brown eyes, 'But *how fulfilled*, Mr Zimuto?' and he repeated tersely, 'Just fulfilled'.

After the Bible Study, when her turn came to pray, the young widow knelt over him and put her small, soft hands on his head and prayed elaborately to the Lord to grant him the fulfillment he desired. Later, when they were enjoying tea and cake, she told him her name was Joyce and invited him to join their church, saying that she taught one of his novels at a local teachers' college. Flattered, he fetched a copy of his latest work and autographed it for her. She promised to invite him to give a talk to her students. (Subsequently he learnt that she had gone to the UK to work as a nurse aide in an old people's home.)

'The Lord is great!' testified a second woman, replete with sponge sandwich. 'Just imagine. There's this guy at our office with a whopping nine O-level passes, distinctions too. He joined the company as tea-boy and enlisted in our lunch-time prayer group. We prayed with him every day. After three months, he was promoted to messenger. Imagine! His parents were both seriously ill, with AIDS. We prayed for them too, but the Good Lord decided their time had come. Still, we prayed and prayed and – can you believe it? – the department of human resources announced that it was availing him of a company truck to ferry his father's body to Mount Darwin for burial, Praise the Lord!'

'Praise the Lord!' chorused the others.

'Praise the Lord!' began a third. 'I was a secretary for twelve years in my firm. I was passed by for many promotions and I could have left. I very nearly did. Then a vacancy arose for a secretarial supervisor. I applied for the post. There were five others in the firm vying for the position, but they were all my juniors. I was the oldest and most experienced of the lot. There were forty-three outside applications. The night before the interview, I prayed till five in the morning. So I was sort of in a trance at the interview and I can't remember what I said. The Lord simply spoke for me, put the right words into my mouth. I got the job. Yes, the Lord said to the other forty-seven applicants, "You are not worthy of the post, because you are women of little faith. I reserve this job for Vhu because she is patient and faithful." Like good old Job in the Old Testament, I was rewarded. I got the job, praise the Lord!'

'Praise the Lord!'

Another of the women asked for Godfrey's cellphone number and said she was writing a collection of modern parables and she would need his help to complete it. Meantime, Vhaidha blinked into her mug of tea, nibbled at her cake and tapped at the red carpet with the heel of her shoe. Afterwards, she brought out bottles of her homemade peanut butter to sell to them.

Godfrey never prayed with them again.

5

I had slowly evolved. I was another person, another creature, constantly searching for new outlines. I had over half a century metamorphosed into the larva of another identity, another being, waiting to burst out of my cocoon. Godfrey Zimuto was me and he wasn't me. Those who were lax often mistook us for the same person. Perhaps he was a twin, sibling, cousin, the boy from next door or just my hapless namesake. Our genealogy might have been the same, but our genes were dissimilar. Godfrey changed first names and surnames like clothes and in such a desultory manner that he sometimes dismayed me. We wore the same size, so we often swopped garments, and I changed appearances too. We were both chameleons, responding conveniently to different environs. I had told his story so often, and sometimes so accurately, to increasingly weary audiences, and he had recounted rumours of me with a vengeance. Incurable raconteurs, we had also raided other people's tales. Together we had crafted, exaggerated and embellished our existences till our two lives and those of our victims blended into one seamless fiction.

For half a century, I'd been searching for a voice. I fought Godfrey for the fiction prize and he hit back. We quarrelled and patched up, patched up and quarrelled. I wanted to break free from him, from the invisible umbilical cord that joined us together, nourishing and yet stifling us. I wanted to get out of myself and be my own man.

We existed at different times and phases, yet we were always alive together in shifting time zones, thriving on little contests. There was an incriminating congruence to our secret geometries. He was the little boy kneeling hungrily on the grass in the huge white tent; I was his redeemed sibling feasting on a doughnut and cream soda and helping our mother blow at the recalcitrant wood stove. I was the little newborn baby squirming beneath baptismal water; he was the bright twelve-year-old parroting his lines to an unforgiving catechist. He was the teenager eagerly tasting unleavened bread and sipping that first little glass of wine yechirairo. I was his cousin rebuking Baba Mebo's shameless parable of the man who could speak many languages but beat up his wife. He was the Form 1 zealot scribbling insipid rhyme-star poems at prep time, commanding Alice the Temptress to get out of his righteous path and expecting to be WOW'd by Mkoma Billet's Week of Witness surprise; I was his namesake chiding his precociousness and foolish, angry disappointment. Together we somehow colluded and condemned Billet for his narrow interpretation of Okara's poem,

173

his engaging in premarital sex, for staging a rushed marriage to save
face. We wrestled girlfriends from each other. But when I, in turn,
married Vhaidha in very similar, if not worse, circumstances, I thought
I heard Brother Billet chuckle, 'Do as I say, silly, not as I do!' My
namesake slated my hypocrisy, insisted we could not blame Mkoma
Billet forever, or for anything for that matter, and we squabbled for
weeks. After that Godfrey and I parted ways. We had grown too big
for each other, knew and threatened one another too much. We had
different callings – careers, anyway. Our lives, which had hitherto
often paralleled or intersected with each other, skimmed away at a
tangent. Our histories, ancestries and experiences strove to unite us
but we waltzed away to separate destinies. I blundered into an early
marriage; he remained the scornful, eternal bachelor, a man free to
possibilities. Now, without him, without Godfrey to anchor me, to act
as my foil, to heckle me into giving an ear to my wife and the other
women who came to my house on the avowed mission to save my
soul, to heed the cautionary hubbub of other voices around me, in the
world's streets and avenues, in the pubs, in workplaces, I was a dead
meteor hurtling through a desolate universe, unable to stop, to change
course, or to relate. I was on my own, plunging out of orbit into the
dark empty void called the future, waiting to crash into some unknown
star.

To burn out.

6

'What have you got *against* yourself?' Mike demands, over his third
beer. I've often seen him here with women. I'm sure I've met him
somewhere before, but I can't remember where. Of late, a miscellany
of grave faces peer into mine with the often naïve intention to prise out
my soul, people know me and I do not know them, it is no longer wise
for me to take chances with strangers. I wonder what has made me
decide to engage with this loquacious individual, why he has picked
on me on this boisterous Saturday night.

'You think you're so ruthless at exposing yourself to the world, but to what end? What do you *believe* in?' he demands, fat round eyes twinkling with accusation.

'Why does that concern you?'

'Because you're as hollow as a gourd. You just drift from one day to the next like a leaf in the wind. What have you got against *God* and our *church*?'

'Which church?'

'God's entire mission.'

'Is that the name of another of your new churches?'

'Listen to you, blaspheming against God. You know which church I'm talking about, man.'

'If I'm blaspheming then what would you say you're doing, getting roaring drunk and making passes at every girl who walks in?'

'God never forbade that. He took Woman out of Man's rib. He created Woman for the gratification of Man, so He never really disapproves of male lust, which is natural. It leads to procreation which is God's will.'

'You chauvinist! You believe that folklore – Adam and Eve and the Serpent. I suppose you believe Woman led to Man's eternal downfall. You denigrate women...'

'You call the good book "folklore"!'

'So you believe the earth was created in seven days; that you were fashioned out of clay and cursed to be pot-black because some son of a Jew derided his drunken, disrobed father and was banished to toil in darkest Africa? That the world's multifarious languages resulted from the so-called Tower of Babel? That Noah's ark was large enough to house a pair of every creature on earth, dinosaurs, elephants, whales? That Judas was black? What happened to evolution? And where were the forefathers of Nehanda and Chaminuka all the while? What happened to our own black folklore?'

'Look who's a racist now. I might be a chauvinist, but I'm saved.'

'Is that what they teach you in your church? Your religion stirs up so many chauvinisms...'

'You're saying so.'

'Do you make passes at every woman in your church?'

'If they throw themselves at me, and there's room to manoeuvre. There's no harm in indulging the flesh as long as you repent. The flesh is fallible.'

'You're a hypocrite. I've met many people who attend your services just to seek out new partners. How many married women in your church have you gone out with?'

'Quite a few, I'd say.'

'Have you taken your infamous pastor's wife, too?'

'Don't mock my church? You're nothing.'

'I have my life. You church people only cause problems.'

'How?'

'The world's worst problems today are caused by three main things: greed, racism and religion. Look at The Middle East, Iran, Afghanistan, Pakistan, India, Ireland and even North, North East and West Africa. *Everywhere!* Religious fanatics, from *both* sides of the divide, whether old or new, are selfish and a danger to humanity. If there was no religion, people thoughout the world would live happily together. Look at Osama bin Laden and other extremists. The greatest threat to the world today is a full-scale war between Islam and Christianity.'

'You're blaspheming again. I suppose you'll add, like John Lennon, that we should do away with national boundaries.'

'If you guys can't do without boundaries on earth, however will you manage in heaven?'

'There are no boundaries in heaven. Heaven is a state of unbounded space.'

'I suppose you'll all congregate in a vacuum. Thousands of billions upon billions of humanoids, black, brown, yellow, white; souls from several thousand millennia ago and cultures right down to our ancestors, the apes. And we mustn't forget the angels, birds, insects and animals. But won't the lions eat the little lambs in heaven, Mike?'

'Don't be silly!'

'And what will you eat every day once you're there? Manna, I suppose. Will there be any special menus for carnivores or vegetarians or you will all have the same fare?'

'You don't understand. In heaven, souls feed on The Word, the

176

Spirit and not on contaminated earthly food.'

'Will there be separate dorms for males, females, children, married couples, different cultures, different races? Will loving couples and families be allowed to reunite? Will there be uniforms, provisions, timetables, languages, translators? Will the inmates be issued with passes, to, say, revisit the earth as ghosts or avenging spirits or will there be no earth left to visit? Why do some people return back to earth as spirits, Mike? Who lets them out? What if the world explodes in a nuclear holocaust when some moron presses one of those little red buttons scattered all over the globe? Will there be a separate judgement day for each individual killed that day? Have you heard of the prophecies of Nostradamus? Or will there be a new war against Satan? Or will the devil and his archangels be too busy roasting their countless guests? And why should God allow his children to be roasted? If I, a creature of flesh and blood, can forgive my son for pinching forty dollars from my wardrobe, why should God want to preach forgiveness and vengefully destroy the world he's said to have created? If your Good Book say, only 144,000 souls will be admitted to heaven is there any point in striving for admission?'

'You can't be serious!'

'Of course, I'm not. I'm pulling your leg. Don't you guys have *any* sense of humour'

'Oh, shit!'

'And what will the inmates of Heaven do in eternity? Sing, pray, testify, I suppose. Doesn't God ever get tired of all this praise? This worship. Come again. Forever? Forever, forever, forever... Say that again, forever, forever, forever...'

'Shut up!'

'Forever, forever, forever, forever, forever, forever, forever, forever, forever, forever, forever, forever, forever, forever, forever, forever, forever, forever, till we down all the beers in this bar and the national breweries run dry, till this watch stops and I buy a new one, till every tree on this earth is pulped into paper and the oceans turn into ink and every literate person on earth reiterates the words FOREVER, FOREVER, FOREVER, till all the paper in the world is covered with

with human scrawl, FOREVER, FOREVER, FOREVER, FOREVER, FOREVER...'

'You're nuts!'

'FOREVER, FOREVER, FOREVER till all voices fade and dissolve into air, till all the trees and flowers die and the rivers and oceans dry up and rock crumbles to dust and the sun and stars burn out and the earth shrivels to nothing and all the brimstone in all the galaxies burns out and the sun, the stars and the moon switch themselves out and all matter is reduced to dust, and dust to nothingness, FOREVER, FOREVER, FOREVER, TILL WHEN? TILL WHEN? TILL WHEN? WHEN? WHEN? WHEN WHEN WHEN WHEN WHEN WHEN WHEN WHEN WHEN WHEN WHEN WHEN WHEN...'

'You're right out of your mind!'

'But wait, Mike. That's only the *Christian* heaven, you see. What about the heavens of *other* religions, Islam, Hindu, Sikh, African, Ibo, Yoruba, Shona, Zulu ... etcetera? Will they exist in a parallel state, or in sequence, or in competition? What about religions that espouse reincarnation, the animists, Zen, atheists, traditionalists? Your own traditional Shona beliefs?'

'But you don't even believe in them.'

'There are people who do.'

'You believe in nothing but yourself.'

'You and your churches do. You don't believe anyone else is right. You've completely blinkered yourselves to other visions of existence.'

'I've heard about your stupid books. You aren't even atheist. You're the biggest egoist that ever walked the face of this earth. '

'I don't know about that. I don't hate God. I think God is some inscrutable force that created and controls the universe. A force even larger than all religions together can begin to comprehend. Two centuries ago who would have dreamt that man would one day set foot on the moon? Was that predicted in your good books? What new knowledge will science bring us in the future? All I know is that I hate churches that thrive on fear, deceit, blind trust, greed and folly. The opium of the masses, indeed!'

'You dare call us "masses"! You think you're very smart. You're nothing, nobody, I tell you. You don't even deserve the wife you had. What do you have against *her*?'

I now realise Mike might have been one of the un-wily recipients of my bar-room tirades against matrimony. 'Don't talk about that woman,' I say, grimly.

'Why shouldn't I? I know now why she left you.'

'It's none of your business. For your own information, she didn't leave me, my wife left of her own accord, held captive by your pastors, I suppose.'

'Because you couldn't keep her captive yourself, you fool. If I told you what I know about her you'd hang yourself, poor soul.'

'I don't want to know.'

'She talked about you, about what a wreck you are.'

'Go on, then.'

'Okay, you asked for this. She and I used to be in the same evening prayer group. Once, when she was still with you, I decided to give her a lift to the meeting. I parked at your gate and hooted. Then you came up the road and parked behind me and I asked, "Is Vhaidha in?"'

'I remember! So it was you! So, you go to the same church!'

'I said, "Is Vhaidha in?" and you know what you said? You said, "Fuck off from my gate, you moron!" and I laughed and drove away. I'll never forget that, you, a *sascam*, calling *me* a moron!'

'If you choose to behave like one at another man's gate then you'll be treated as one.'

'What wrong did I do? Vhaida had asked me to pick her up. Are you calling me a moron again?'

'Yes, if you insist on behaving like one. But you're always welcome to eat my vomit if you wish.'

'Eat your *what*? What did you say?'

Mike grabs a stool and slams it at my drink. He slams it again and again at the bar; the upward thrust of its legs smash the glass panel above the counter; the vibration knocks over a dozen bottles of spirits and sends them exploding onto the floor. I duck. A hush has fallen over the bar and Miriam, the bartender, creeps into a corner. The bar manager and the bouncers freeze in the doorway.

Mike throws off his coat and staggers towards me. He's breathing like a bull and his eyes are ablaze. A bottle of rare whisky tumbles from the shelf and crashes onto the floor. I stand up and lean back, looking for a way to escape.

Mike lunges at me, hands balled into crude fists, face contorted into a hideous mask of unforgiving Neanderthal rage.

'What did you say?' he hisses like a serpent, his spittle shooting into my face.

I'm already dead from his venom.

Forever dead.